DRAGON'S GIFT

RED PLANET DRAGONS OF TAJSS BOOK TWELVE

MIRANDA MARTIN

CONTENTS

1

MAEVE

The rising double red suns cause the drifting sands to glint and glimmer. Tiny rainbows and waves of heat dance across the distant dunes. It's pretty, really, if only it wasn't so blasted hot. When I stretch my arms over my head and lean from side to side, my back cracks loudly.

"Oh," I exclaim. Deep breath in and blow it out. The surprise is worse than the momentary discomfort. "It's going to be a good day."

I'm talking to myself, but I don't care. I like to fix my ideas out loud. It seems to work. Sets the direction and all that. I've always believed the day is what you make of it, and I choose to make each day the best I can.

Inhaling the hot air, letting it out slowly, and considering what's to come as I watch the suns rise, a shadow catches my eye. It looks like something is growing out there. That piques my curiosity and draws me forward, away from the protective wall around the caves.

I'm not stupid. I know everything on the planet is going to try to kill me, so I move forward cautiously, alert for the slightest of hints that this is a bad idea. Anything growing outside the garden that is so carefully tended inside the walls is worthy of investigation, in my opinion at least.

It's been a roller coaster ride since we crashed here. Some good, some bad, but overall, things are getting better. Finding and joining with the Tribe here at the Caves has been a big step up from living in the tunnel under Annabel's tyrannical fits.

Finding the other survivors was a huge improvement. I know some of my fellow humans are still hung up on being "rescued," but the majority of us have come to terms with our situation. There will be no rescue. Thinking otherwise was ridiculous, in my opinion, in the first place. There is a reason our ancestors left Earth. It's not like they were wanted there. If they had been, they wouldn't have boarded a generation ship headed for a destination they knew they would never see. That's common sense to me.

Sure, life here isn't easy, but we are alive. Might as well make the best of it.

The suns are a bit higher now, so I draw closer to the shadow, and it takes on color, shades of red with hints of orange. It has diamond-shaped leaves that spread out across the sand. Grinning, I crouch down and study it, watching to see if it does anything. This is Tajss. God only knows what this thing's defenses are.

Behind me I hear the Tribe stirring to life on the other side of the protective wall that blocks off the living area from the outside. I'll need to go in soon, but right now this plant has my attention. No clue if it will even be edible, not my area of expertise, but we have people for that. I'm only gathering data.

"What are you doing!" a deep, bass voice yells, rolling across the loose sand.

"Wha-!" I exclaim, jumping and turning so I land facing the source.

My heart pounds in my throat, and I'm shaking with a strange mix of fear and anger.

Padraig. Ugh. The big, oversized Zmaj stands glaring. His massive, trunk-like arms are raised and aimed at me. His are wings spread and his tail is swinging back and forth in agitation.

"Taking my morning constitutional, you?" I ask, full on snark rising in response to both the scare he gave me and my general irritation at being yelled at.

"You can't be out here," he hisses. "It isn't safe, not authorized, no, this cannot be. Get inside, now."

"Authorized?" I ask, arching an eyebrow. "Seriously?"

"Yes," he hisses, moving closer.

"You're serious," I say, shaking my head.

"Of course," he says, looking past me. "It's not safe. Now we have invaders and Tajss is not safe for…"

He trails off, not having to finish the thought. My hackles rise in response, anger pulsing through my body like a rumbling bass drum. He did not go there. Staring at him, utter disbelief stunning me to silence, I wait for him to finish speaking.

"For?" I ask, when he doesn't.

That pulls his attention back to me. He stares, his mouth slightly open, his eyes wide in obvious surprise.

"A female," he says, shaking his head. "A human."

"Which is it?" I ask, hands on hips. "A human? Or a female?"

"Both," he says, dropping his arms to his sides, his wings closing. "We must get behind the wall, now."

It's not what he's saying that is pissing me off, it's how he is saying it. It seems clear as day to me that his actual

3

problem is that I'm a girl. I don't know what his issue is, but of all the Zmaj I've met, he's the most surly, irritating, and hardest to get along with. He's an unnecessarily rude Dragon.

"And what if I say no?" I ask, glaring.

The surprise is so obvious on his face I have to suppress a laugh. I don't think it possibly occurred to him that I can have my own consideration or thoughts. He may be an alien Dragon but that doesn't stop him from being a male chauvinist pig.

"It's not safe," he repeats, as if that is an answer to my question.

He motions back towards the gate looking from it to me.

"And?"

"And? What? It's not safe," he repeats, but his voice has lost its edge now.

"You're oblivious and an idiot," I say, stomping past him.

"Oblivious?" he asks from behind me.

"Yes!" I shout, spinning on my heel to face him.

I'm rewarded by him taking a step back, raising his hands before him, palms out, making a downward patting motion as if he's trying to calm me. Rewarded yes, but it pisses me off even more.

"Do not try to calm me down!" I shout. "You and your patriarchal ideals–I'm not a delicate flower. I was totally fine. I'm not stupid, and I don't need you protecting my every move."

Padraig's brow furrows, he shakes his head, still patting the air with his hands.

"It's not safe," he repeats, but I hear the numbness in his words. He's clinging to his idea, not listening to what I say.

"Gah!" I exclaim, spinning again and storming through the gate, heading back behind the wall.

Let him stand out there in the sand until he gets a clue. This was a good day. Was, until he interrupted it. Why is it always him? He's such a total jerk. Always with his superior attitude and grabbing control. Heck, I've even seen him doing with the other Zmaj. He's a thundercloud on a perfect sunny day, coming to ruin everyone's good time.

Stopping inside the wall I take a deep breath, trying to let it go. It's done, Maeve, calm down. I'm not going to let him, of all people, ruin the rest of my day. Nope, not going to do it.

I hope.

Ugh. It's still there. An irritation boiling inside my guts that isn't going anywhere. This happens all the time, once something pisses me off, I can't let it go. I wish I could, but it will sit there and boil in my thoughts like a festering wound. The only solution is to get busy with something else.

Most everyone seems to be awake and moving now. People are moving up and down the ramp to the small caves that serve as our personal spaces and even more people are out tending the garden. Errol is working at his small shop.

I'm supposed to be gathering vegetables and helping prep them for storage and meals but instead of heading to the large garden that stretches out from the massive main cave in the cliff that is our home, I walk over towards his shop.

"How's it going?" I ask, as I approach.

He has a massive machine thing that he's been building sitting on the sand next to a table filled with parts and pieces of meteorite glass.

"Good," Errol says, glancing up and smiling. "I'm close... I think."

He leans in close to the machine, pressing a piece of glass into it, and sparks leap out.

"Ouch," he exclaims dancing backwards.

"Oh, you okay?" I ask.

He inspects his fingers closely then shakes his head. "Yeah."

"Right, well I'll leave you to it."

"Thanks," he says, distracted by what he's working on.

Suppressing an absolutely irrational giggle, I leave him to his work. I don't know why I find it funny, it's certainly not his pain, but the look on his face was hysterical. It does serve to take my thoughts off of Padraig, so I give Errol a silent thank you for that.

I do my duties working with the others, spending my time harvesting the vegetables that are ready, clearing gunk from the irrigation canals. It's necessary work, if a bit boring. It's easy to lose myself in the rhythm of it and carry on getting things done.

Even this early in the morning, it's hot. By the time I fill my crate with harvested veggies, sweat is pouring off of me like a fricking waterfall. Epis may adjust my body to survive, but it doesn't make the heat enjoyable by any means.

Straightening, I put my hands on my lower back and stretch, trying to ease the tension in my sore muscles. The suns are well above the horizon now, beating down on us in their never-ending attack. I wipe sweat from my brow, then pick up my box of vegetables.

"Wow, you got done fast," Olivia says, glancing over.

"It's easier when I don't have the extra distraction," I reply, smiling and glancing over at Zoe, who is toddling down the carefully cultivated rows of vegetables inspecting each one carefully before going to the next.

"Yeah," Olivia laughs. "She does add a bit of randomness to the day."

Zoe glances over at us and smiles. My heart swells pushing out the last bits of irritation that Padraig had created in me. How can you not have hope when you look into her sweet face? Her blue eyes sparkle brightly, her scales cast tiny rainbows reflecting the sun, and the warm wind stirs her red hair.

"Mommy," she says.

"Yes, my love," Olivia replies.

"I have a question, Mommy," Zoe says.

"What is your question?" Olivia asks.

"How do these grow so straight?" Zoe asks, pointing at the rows of plants.

"Because we make them," Olivia answers. "See, this is how we planted them."

Olivia crouches down next to Zoe and points out the rows.

"Oh," Zoe says. She leans down and inspects the dirt carefully. "I see."

"Of course you do," Olivia says. "My brilliant little baby."

"I love you mommy," Zoe says.

Olivia beams with pride, and how can I blame her? Zoe is brilliant, beautiful, but she and all of the babies are so much more than that. They represent hope.

There's nothing to compare it to. It is one of those subtle things that I don't think anyone actually realized was on our minds after we had crashed. That subtle understanding that we would be the end of our race. The Zmaj understood it much better than we did, they had years and years to come to terms with it. It was also more obvious for them, since there were no Zmaj females left.

Thinking about that, it becomes obvious that our Zmaj saviors were also saved by us. We need each other in a beautiful kind of symmetry. Olivia and Zoe continue their conversation as I turn and walk towards the main cave with the fruit of my labor.

The day seems brighter, again, as it should. The dark cloud that Padraig had cast over it is gone. A song starts playing in my head as I walk along. It's an old earth show tune from one of my favorite Vids from back on the ship. I hum along to it as I walk.

"I told you to leave that alone," an unmistakable deep voice booms, jerking me out of my thoughts.

Padraig towers over Samil who is cowering before him.

"Sorry," Samil says, shaking his head and holding his hands out palms up into submission.

"Fix it," Padraig growls.

I can't believe how far he takes his dominating male persona. It irritates me in ways I can't even put into words. Glaring, I debate whether I want to get involved in this or not. As if he senses me, Padraig notices me and his eyes lock on mine.

Anger flares white hot inside me, and my decision is taken out of my hands by the irrationality of how pissed I am. I storm over to him, dropping the box of vegetables on my way.

"What is your malfunction?" I ask, glaring up to try and meet his eyes.

"What?" he asks, confusion on his face as he takes a step back from my verbal assault.

"Your malfunction? Why can't you be nice? Get along?"

"He broke the rules," Padraig says, shaking his head. "He knows better, we must have rules."

"Must we? Are we slaves to these rules? Can we not think for ourselves? Make new choices as the situation calls for it?"

I have no idea what Samil did, and at this point I don't care. It's not about Samil any longer, it's about me, and him yelling at me this morning.

"No?" he answers but the question in his words is apparent.

His wings rustle behind him but his tail is still. He takes another step backwards and the tinge of color on his scale shifts taking on a bluish hue.

"No? Is that a question? Can we think or not?" I ask, pressing my attack.

"I'll fix it, it's my fault," Samil says, stepping into my peripheral vision.

"Sure, you do that," I snap at him, glaring at Padraig. "And you…"

I put my finger under Padraig's chin then accent my words by poking him in the chest.

"Get over yourself. Learn to be nice," I say.

"I—" he starts but I cut him off with my glare. His mouth snaps shut.

"Right," I say, turning and walking back to my vegetables, steaming once again. Jerking them off the ground I carry them away, feeling the two Zmaj males' stares on my back as I leave.

Let them stare. I've had my fill of Padraig's rudeness. He's completely overbearing and takes the whole manly man thing to a new, ridiculous level.

Storming into the kitchen area I slam the box down on the table, gripping it so tight my knuckles are white.

"Gah!" I exclaim, venting the frustration and anger pounding in my chest.

Delilah looks up from the vegetables she is preparing. I try to will myself to let go of the box, but there's a moment where my clenched hands refuse to obey. My heart pounds and my breathing is shallow.

"Who pissed you off?" Delilah asks, placing a hand over mine.

I take a look at her calm, dark chocolate eyes, and then I take a deep breath and exhale it slowly, pushing the anger out along with it. She smiles, lighting up her face and helping to lift the heaviness off of me.

"Padraig," I say, shaking my head.

"Again?" She laughs.

"He's so frustrating," I snap.

"And sexy," she grins.

"You've got to be kidding me," I say, shaking my head. "He's entirely too…"

Too what? I ask myself. *Irritating, demanding, masculine, manly, muscled. No, stop that!*

Delilah laughs at my pause.

"Yeah?" She asks, arching an eyebrow.

"No way," I say. "No, not going to happen, no way."

"Well, it is what it is. Of course, if you're not interested, I'm sure one of the other girls will be," she says.

There's an almost instantaneous stabbing pain in my chest. I stare into the distance, trying to figure out what the hell is wrong with me. I can't possibly be interested in him. He's irritating. Frustrating. Agitating. I think I could go on and on with adjectives to describe how much he pisses me off.

Delilah watches with delight in her eyes. The smile never leaves her face, even as she picks her knife back up and returns to cleaning the vegetables. Silent, debating internally, I grab a knife and help her.

"He's a jerk," I say at last.

"He's a man," Delilah answers.

"All men are jerks," I say.

"Hmmm," she replies.

"They're not, I guess," I counter my own thought, my voice cracking. Delilah arches an eyebrow at me. "Samil is nice."

"Sure," she responds, entirely too agreeable.

"You're impossible," I laugh at my own absurdity.

The heaviness of my mood is lifting, which I'm glad for. Sometimes, no matter how hard I try, I have a hard time letting go of things. We fall into an easy rhythm of prepping vegetables and filling the pot. Our conversation turns light, and I push all thoughts of Padraig aside.

"Oh!" I exclaim. "What time is it?"

I look around wishing, not for the first time, that we had some method of telling time here on Tajss.

"Midmorning," Delilah answers.

"I totally forgot, I'm supposed to get the meteorite glass from the mining village," I say, dropping the knife and rushing out of the prep area.

As soon as I emerge from the caves, the oppressive heat slams into me almost as if it's a wall of its own. My body responds with an immediate sheen of sweat. Racing past other members of the tribe working, I head for the wall and the gate through it.

I see Melchior talking with one of the miners by the wall as I approach, but I don't see the shipment that I'm supposed to be receiving.

"Where is it? I ask, breathless, as I skid to a stop in a spray of loose sand.

The two men look at me in surprise.

"Where is what?" Melchior asks.

"The shipment," I say, looking around as if it might magically appear in my site.

"Padraig already took it," Melchior responds.

It's immediate, I'm seeing red. All the anger that I had let go of is back with renewed force. My heart is a bass drum as I turn on my heel and stomp after the Zmaj. He had no right. This was my job. Mr. We-have-to-have-rules-and-they-must-be-obeyed can't go around breaking them himself. I don't think there is anything in the world that pisses me off more than a hypocrite.

I spot him at his forge working on some metal. The loud clanging of his hammer beating down on the hot iron rings in my ears. It accents the rush of blood in my ears. I come to a stop in front of him, put my hands on my hips, and glare until he stops the swing of his hammer. He looks at me with confusion on his face and a frown.

"Where do you get off?" I say through gritted teeth.

He tilts his head to one side, his lips part, his tail shifts across the loose sand.

"I do not understand," he replies.

"That was my job! Where is the glass?"

"Errol requested it," he responds, shaking his head side-to-side.

"I know that," I say. "It was my job to deliver it."

"I was helping," he says, shrugging.

"Did I ask for your help?" I snap.

"No?" He says, sounding more like a question. "But it is help, you do not have to ask for my help."

"If I want your help, I will ask for it," I yell.

"I do not understand," he says, staring at me as if I have grown a second head.

"Of course you don't," I say, throwing my hands up in the air with frustration. "You're just the big man. You've got it all under control. Keep us women in our place."

"That is not what I meant," he says. "I was helping. Why is this a problem?"

"Gah!" I exclaim, unable to form words.

We stare at each other, neither of us willing to blink. He's not going to bend and neither am I. I don't know what it is about him that gets under my skin, but it's more than I can stand. Especially right now. His overt masculinity and his driving need to apparently be the big alpha on campus rubs me the wrong way.

Other people have stopped and are watching our

confrontation. Suddenly I feel awkward and out of place. I know, rationally, that I am overreacting to his action. That does nothing to actually settle my temper, but it does give me pause.

"Don't take my jobs from me, got it?" I ask.

"As you wish," he says, showing no signs of anger.

"Good," I say, turning away from him. "Nothing to see here!" I yell at the gawking onlookers.

My embarrassment is now complete. I know I just made a huge fool of myself, but there's nothing for it now. The burning in my cheeks and my shortness of breath only make it worse. I make haste back to Delilah so that I can hide my disgrace.

It would have been so much better if he had responded with anger too. It would've made me feel justified. There is that niggling part of my brain telling me that he really did only want to help. I should accept that. The thing is, I would if it was anybody but him. What is it about him that makes me react this way?

Sighing, I give up trying to figure it out. At this point I don't know.

The rest of the day passes quickly, and fortunately, I am able to avoid running into Padraig again. As we all sit down to dinner there is no sign of him. I'm thankful for this, because if I saw him, I would probably feel a strong urge to apologize. I'm not ready for that.

"I really can't stand the hyper masculinity thing," I say to Delilah and Fallon.

"Maybe that is the only way he knows how to be," Fallon says.

"The Zmaj survive off the strength of their masculinity," Delilah says. "It's part of their nature."

"The other men don't act like him," I say.

"Don't they?" Delilah asks, arching one perfect eyebrow.

13

I snap my mouth shut thinking about what she said. Mostly, we're both right. None of the other Zmaj are as irritating as Padraig. Yes, they all have that masculine, need to dominate streak, but they don't carry it as far as he does. I find them to be much more tolerable.

Following smiles with a sage look on her face as if she knows something the rest of us don't, but she doesn't say anything.

"Okay," I sigh. "So it's just him. He really gets under my skin."

"Sometimes, that can be a good thing," Fallon says, smirking.

"No way," I say, rolling my eyes, but my cheeks burn hot.

I can't admit, even to my closest friends here, that I have had such thoughts about him. I don't even want to admit it to myself. He is a very good-looking man. Well, an alien Dragon man, but still a man. Strong, muscular, but more than that, he has kind eyes. That's probably the biggest thing I don't want to admit to, that I find his eyes fascinating. There is a depth to them that is intriguing.

"Never say never," Delilah says, a grin spreading across her face.

"Sure," I snort.

Penelope slides into a seat next to us, leaning over her swelling belly to rest her elbow on the table.

"Hi," we all welcome her, but I'm particularly glad for the change of topic.

"I've been thinking," she says, "and I'd like to hear your thoughts."

"About?" Delilah asks.

"Christmas," she says.

"What?" I ask, surprised.

"Christmas," she repeats, covering her stomach with an arm.

"Huh," Fallon says.

"Yeah?" Penelope asks.

"Well... I guess... what about it?" Delilah says.

"We've been here a long time now, and this is our home," she's gazing at her stomach, rubbing it with one hand. "Up till now it's all been about surviving. I think it's time we focus on living too."

Delilah, Fallon, and I exchange a long look. She's right, really. I've only been here at the Tribe for a short time, but we have been on Tajss for a long time. The furthest thing from my mind has been celebrating holidays or anything else but it would be nice.

Penelope watches us, her emerald eyes flashing brightly, catching the flames of the candle. A half-smile rests easily on her lips while she lets us process the idea.

"Why not?" Delilah says. "We have kids now and everything."

"I think it's a good idea," Fallon says. "I like it."

"I do too," I decide. "What do we need to do to make it happen?"

"I've been thinking about that," Penelope says. "We've lost track of the days and none of us have any kind of calendar. The ones we had wouldn't really work for Tajss anyway, they were based off Earth days, which is totally different here."

"Right," I nod along with her logic.

"So basically, we pick a day. One day we're going to designate as Christmas. A day to celebrate giving, sharing, and caring for one another. All the great things that Christmas represents, no matter what your faith or belief may be," she continues.

"That's really quite brilliant," Fallon says, smiling. "Have you talked with the others yet?"

"Some," she says. "I'm gauging interest."

"I'm in," Delilah says. "We can even make a calendar of

sorts. It'd be nice to have some measure of the passing of time. Give life more a sense of normalcy."

"Good idea," I say.

"Thanks!" she says, climbing to her feet and walking away.

"I have been led to understand that Errol is making progress on getting his new contraption to work," Fallon says.

"Oh, that would be great," I say, smiling.

"Who knows," Delilah says. "One day maybe we can be a real city too."

The reference to the city is joking but carries a weight with it. There is a running desire among the tribe to make sure that they can be fully self-sufficient. Apparently, there was tension with the city at some point that is not forgotten even if it is almost never spoken of out loud.

It makes me think of Annabelle and her tyrannical rule. That is the past, the future is ahead of us, and the now is okay. After finishing my food, I rise and offer to take my friends' plates as well. They thank me, and I carry them to the wash station.

The double suns are setting, casting long shadows. After I wash our plates, I look around for something to do until it's time for bed and see Sarah loading candles into a box.

"Hey," I say, walking up to her.

"Hi," she says, pausing to wipe her brow.

"Where to with this batch?" I ask, motioning the box.

"Those are for Errol," she says, rolling her neck and rubbing at her shoulders.

"Want me to take it for you?" I ask.

"Would you?" she asks, relief flooding her face.

"Sure!" I say, happy to help.

I grab up the box, surprised at its weight, and walk out of the main cave where the candle making happens, towards

Errol's work area. I almost wish I hadn't offered or had asked for help. This thing is really heavy. My arms burn with effort as I struggle to carry it. Dusk lies heavily over the back of the cave, and my eyes aren't adjusting very fast. I'm so focused on carrying the crate that I bump into someone who grunts, so it's obviously a Zmaj, but my heart sinks when he turns, and I see it's Padraig.

Of all the Zmaj on this interminable planet for me to bump into!

He stares at me for a long moment, the two of us silently squaring each other up. His eyes drop to the box and he motions towards it, wordlessly offering to carry it.

Relief wars with my desire to not let him have an opportunity to prove his manhood, but that irrational thought is quickly overcome by the burning in my arms. I nod and he takes the box. We walk to Errol's in an uneasy silence. He carries the box as if it weighs nothing, which it probably does to him. His arms are massive, bulging affairs. A body builder couldn't be prouder of their build. Grudgingly I admit it's both impressive and kind of sexy. Kind of, let's not push it. He's still abrasive which takes points away.

Errol is at a worktable doing something with a piece of meteorite glass and barely looks up as we walk in.

"Put it there, please," he says, glancing over his shoulder before returning his attention to his work.

Padraig sets the box down, wordlessly, then I follow him out of the workshop. He stops, not quite staring at me, and I shift from one foot to the other trying to figure out what to say.

"Thanks," I offer.

"Anytime," he says, looking at my feet. The awkward moment stretches. "Have a good night."

He turns and walks.

"You too," I call after his retreating form.

A moment of kindness. One, yes, but a moment of him not being an aggressive jerk igniting my curiosity. Is there more to him than the gruff exterior? Maybe? Okay, he's not a hundred percent bonehead. Eighty-five percent.

Laughing to myself as I yawn, I go to bed, letting all things of the day go, for now.

2

PADRAIG

The scent of food makes my mouth water. I would argue that the best thing the humans have brought to us is their way with food. Before they arrived, we ate dried meats. It was monotonous but what did it matter? We were a doomed race living out our final days. I know most of my brethren are most thankful for the renewed hope and the future that they brought to us. I am too, but the food is remarkable. It has to stand on a similar level.

Scents that I'd never experienced drift across the open air, enticing and teasing my senses, pulling me forward. The communal table is filled. The buzz of morning conversation fills the air and I have to admit there's a sense of satisfaction that comes over me looking at it.

Until I spot Maeve.

My hearts stop, my chest constricts, and my mouth goes dry. She's as beautiful as she is inscrutable. I do not under-stand her or her ways. Why can't she be like so many of the other females? If she was, she'd be perfect.

She's not and it's frustrating. I try to help her, to be a protector, as any male should, but it never goes right with her. No matter what I do or say, it's wrong in her eyes. It makes no sense. She's strange, exotic, and there's no denying the call in my soul to her.

It will never work. She won't accept my help or protection. Our fates are doomed before they start.

Looking up and down the table there's not a single open space to sit except next to her. Closing my eyes, I take two deep breaths, then open them hoping someone will rise and create an opening. Frustratingly, that doesn't happen.

Filling my plate slowly, trying to buy time, I keep the hope of someone rising alive until at last I'm standing there with a full plate of delicious smelling food and no place to sit except next to her. Resigning myself to the situation I walk over and stand silent, waiting for her to acknowledge me.

She turns her head, staring at me. She doesn't say a word, the stare continuing, as if daring me to speak or sit. I meet her stare, refusing to blink or look away. Perhaps this is a human ritual. I'm not sure, I haven't seen any of the other males do this with their mates, but Maeve is different. She wasn't with the other humans. Maybe her tribe is different than theirs, it certainly seems she has her own customs she clings to and I'm doing my best to adjust to them.

"Are you going to sit or stand there staring?" she asks, shaking her head.

Frowning, uncertain if I've won a contest or lost, I take a seat next to her. There are other females at this end of the table and no Zmaj. They're conversing about something, using a word I'm not familiar with. Listening closely to their conversation while eating I repeat the word in my head, trying to grasp its meaning and purpose.

Chrisss-mazzz.

Chrisss-masss.

"There are no trees, well none that would work," the dark female, Delilah says.

"True, we could do something makeshift," Penelope says. "It's what we did on the ship."

"Right," Maeve agrees. "I'm sure we can rig something."

"What about presents? It's not like we can go to the shopping district," Sarah says.

"We'll make them," Penelope says. "That makes them more personal."

Presents. What are presents? I wonder.

They talk faster and faster, growing more excited and animated as the conversation continues. I'm quickly lost in all the words I don't know the meaning of until at last I focus on my food, letting their words flow around me, giving them no attention.

When my plate is empty I stare at it, debating whether to have seconds. It would be an indulgence. My stomach is full and to eat more would be wasteful which makes my decision for me. I take my plate to the wash station and rinse it.

My hearts thump hard when I check the daily duty list and see Maeve and I are to collect meteorite glass. She and the other females are still talking animatedly at the table. She can't know this yet—if she did, I'm certain her mood would not be as happy.

A chance to be alone with her.

The song singing in my blood wars with what I know. She's not interested. Blast everything to nothingness. Why can I not resign myself to the truth?

I can't stop hoping that today will be the day. The day I will prove myself to her, she will see me as a worthy protector, accept me for the role I am meant to play.

Shaking my head as I walk away from the posting, I go and gather my things. After strapping my lochaber to my back and taking a shoulder pack with some basic supplies, I go to the gate and wait. Leaning against the wall gives me a full view of the females finishing their conversation, even if I can't hear them.

She rises, puts her plate away, then walks over to the assignments. Her shoulders drop, she shakes her head, then says something to Delilah. The two of them have a conversation that goes on as the seconds drag.

Maeve shakes her head, throws her hands up in the air, then turns on a heel. She sees me waiting and shakes her head again. Delilah says something else and resolve settles across Maeve's face.

Well, nothing has changed yet.

"Let's go," she says, walking past me without stopping.

Silent, I walk next to her as we leave the safety of the wall enclosed area. I don't mind the silence, it avoids any possibility of my being distracted. This is for the best, I will not let any harm come to her. Her presence alone is distraction enough. No matter how vigilant I am, I cannot help but notice every little thing she does. The way her hips sway as she fights her way up a sand dune. The way her lips part, so full, so lush and inviting.

The moisture that runs down her forehead drips into her eyes and she pauses to wipe it away. I offer her my container of water and she takes it gratefully. I am rewarded with a half-smile. It makes my spirits lift. When she smiles it is brighter than both of the suns in the sky. It lights up her entire face, makes her eyes sparkle with delight, and fills me with a joy I cannot remember ever having felt. All of this from only half a smile. I can only imagine what it would be like if she was to give me a full and truly joyous smile. Perhaps I would explode.

"Thanks," she says, handing the container back to me.

I hook it back on to my belt and nod. The desire to say something is strong but tempered by the fact that I know anything I say will not come out right. My experience with her has taught me well. I am not good with words, never have been, and around her, what little ability I do have with them fails me.

She stares for a long moment as if waiting for me to speak. When I do not, she turns and shields her eyes to look out over the distance.

"I think that over there by that cliff will be a good area to investigate," she says, glancing over her shoulder. "Unless you have a better idea?"

I follow her gaze, closing my protective lenses to filter out the light. She is correct, that does look like a good area. Nodding my agreement, she waits for a further response. I've made up my mind to speak as little as possible, hoping that this approach will lead to a better relationship between us. After the silence stretches to the point of being uncomfortable, she shrugs and starts walking.

The land is rolling dunes, nothing too high or difficult to navigate. Even Maeve is not having too much trouble, unusual for a human. They are not well designed for life on Tajss. The sand shifts in front of us, before it should.

"Stop," I whisper, grabbing her shoulder.

"Wha—" she exclaims but I cut off the word with a hand over her mouth.

Her eyes widen, fury burning in them. She grabs the wrist of my hand covering her mouth and tries to pull it away. It's a futile gesture. Shaking my head, silent, I mouth the word stop to her. This infuriates her more and she swings her right fist, hitting me in the chest.

Frowning I shake my head again, using my free hand to grab her right arm but she swings with her left. The sand shifts again, more this time and now I feel the slight tremor of the ground beneath us. Desperate to make her understand I nod towards the ground, afraid to speak. Any noise could attract the monster passing somewhere below us.

She's smart, stopping her struggle and looking. When she sees what I do she goes dead still, and I remove my hands from her. The ground trembles again, more than before, it's coming closer. Moving slowly, I reach over my shoulder, taking hold of my lochaber.

Potential scenarios play through my thoughts as I prepare for anything. If it attacks, I'll hold its attention while she runs. If it's big, the best, I'll be able to do is buy her time to escape. The tremor becomes a rumble. Any moment now, it could burst through the surface. Tightening my grip on the lochaber, I draw it out of its holder, slowly, silently.

Maeve's face is pale, eyes wide, and moisture pours down her face. Our gazes meet and I smile, nodding. Surprise blossoms in her face, but smartly she doesn't express it in any vocal manner. The rumble softens, becoming a tremor once again. The zemlja is moving on, having found no prey. Its constant hunt continues somewhere away from us.

At last there is nothing. We remain silent for several long minutes past the sensation of the last tremor before letting out sighs of relief.

"I am sorry," I apologize.

"You caught that before I did," she says, shaking her head. "Thank you."

My hearts swell until I'm sure my chest will explode as they've grown so large. The smile across my face cannot be controlled, I have to look away from her brilliant, beautiful eyes.

"Of course," I say. "A male protects the fragile."

"What?" she asks, a sudden sharpness to her tone.

I turn back to her, and confusion sweeps through my thoughts. Her anger is instant and hot, beating against my scales.

"We protect," I say, not understanding.

"Sure," she says. "What did you say after that? Did you call me 'fragile'?"

"You're a female," I say, well aware I'm sinking but completely lost on why.

"I'm not 'fragile,'" she says. "Yes I'm a female, but that doesn't make me weak."

"But," I try to find words, never my strength. Words don't work for me. Steel does, metal that bends and shapes to my will. Other people, words, they don't conform like a good piece of metal.

"No buts," she says, not waiting for me to find what I want to say. "I'm not weak and I won't be treated as if I am. You have strengths, but so do I."

"Of course," I agree. "But you're female."

"So we've established," she says, shaking her head.

"A male protects," I say, struggling to comprehend what I said that was wrong.

"Yeah, sure," she says. "Does that make me weak?"

Holding my hands up, palms to the sky, I shake my head.

"Right," she says. "I'm not weak. Females are not 'less' than males."

"No, you do not understand," I say, desperation rising.

"No, I don't," she agrees.

"Females are," I stop, gathering my thoughts, trying to find the way to say what I want to say. She waits quietly watching. "Treasures."

"Treasures?" she asks.

"Yes," I say.

She stares, and I can't read her face. I'm not sure if the words broke through, said what I want to say or not. Her lips purse, her brow furrows, then she wipes the moisture from her head. Strange sensations bubble in my stomach and core as my hearts pound out each passing moment, waiting.

"You're impossible," she says, shaking her head and turning away.

The words are harsh, but her voice is soft, like the touch of a delicate feather passing over my scales. Before she turned, something in her eyes changed. It may not be much, but it is enough.

"Continue?" I ask, gesturing towards the cliff she had pointed out.

"Sure," she says, not looking at me.

The rest of our trek passes in silence that is not as deep or uneasy as it previously was. Perhaps I said the right thing. Or not.

As we get closer to our destination the sparkle of meteorite glass is clear to see. A sense of pride swells and fills my chest, not for myself but for her. Her brilliance shines through in every little thing she does.

"You were right," I say, intending a compliment.

She shoots me a sharp look, arching an eyebrow making it clear that my words don't have the intended effect.

"Thanks," she responds.

The look on her face, there's something in her eyes that I hope is a warming. Her voice sounded warmer, almost grateful. Am I making headway? I can only hope.

We set to gathering the glass. As we work I watch her, doing my best to not be noticed. She works with a strong focus. All of her attention is on what she is doing. Picking up pieces of meteorite, holding them before her face, closely examining each one before placing it in the bag on her hip. She discards two out of five pieces as not suitable.

The suns have climbed about five degrees when she stops. Following her lead, I also stop and watch, silently, as she takes a long drink of water.

"Is it just me, or is it even hotter today?" She asks.

I look around, trying to decipher what she means. The temperature seems the same as always to me.

"I don't think it's particularly hotter today," I say.

A cloud passes over her face and I know that I have said the wrong thing again. My scales itch and my fingers twitch. Why can I not say the right thing with her?

Words. I never have found them useful. A male is about action, doing, words have always been the realm of others.

"Yeah," she says, shaking her head.

I've killed the conversation. That much is obvious because she goes back to work without looking at me again. Gritting my teeth, I also resume the gathering. Where there had been an easiness between us, I now feel tension. The words turn over and over in my mind as I try to come up with a better solution. Something I could have said that would have made her happy. A sound pulls me out of my thoughts and I freeze. Something is whistling, I'm not familiar with the sound. It's not a predator that I know. Maeve continues working oblivious to the sound. I stand up and tilt my head to one side, focusing on it. Maeve notices and stops as well.

"What is it?" She asks.

I shake my head, uncertain still. The sound is growing louder, and then I realize it's coming from up above. Scanning the sky, I don't see the source.

"Something," I say.

It strikes me what is about to happen. Another meteorite shower!

The burning rocks come out of the suns line which had shielded them from my sight. The first slams into the ground around us sending plumes of dirt and sand into the air. Spreading my wings, I bend my knees and leap for Maeve, intent on protecting her.

A meteorite lands directly behind her. The impact raises a

cloud around us, blinding me. She screams in pain. My red-hot anger flashes out, and the bijass rushes in behind it. Spreading my arms wide I roar, calling for her with wordless sound as rage pounds with every beat of my hearts.

Pain. White-hot, blinding pain in my chest.

"Ah!" I cry out, as the burning passes through my scales, digging in.

Clawing at it with both hands my fingers burn when I touch it and I jerk them back.

"Padraig!" Maeve cries out.

"Maeve!" I scream, the sound of her name ripping my throat.

I'm waving my arms through the dirt and sand cloud, desperately feeling my way towards where I think she was. I touch her. Grabbing, I pull her tight against my chest and hunch over, protectively wrapping my wings around us.

We need shelter, now. The meteorites slam down around us with echoing, booming sounds that assault our ears. I run towards the cliff, moving closer, hoping to find some form of shelter. Something flashes to my left, bright orange and yellow. Searing pain all down my side. Stabbing pains burn but I ignore them. She is all that matters.

Maeve whimpers in my arms. The sound of her pain drives me forward. Half-blind, even my second lenses aren't enough to filter out the dirt and sand in the air. I find the cliff when my head runs into it. A new round of pain, but it's a degree of shelter. This can't last much longer, I hope.

There's nothing more I can do except protect her body with mine. Dropping to my knees, I curl myself protectively around her and enclose my wings around us. The burning rocks beat against the earth. Their assault continues endlessly. My entire world focuses on her as I push past the searing pain. The assault on my scales is almost more than I can handle. My wings are torn and pierced. My scales are compromised under the relentless attack. The bijass thrusts forward in waves, pushing for flight, to run.

I won't give in. I am myself. Together we are stronger. Survival of the Tribe matters. She is Tribe. She matters. She is all that matters.

"We need better shelter," Maeve says, barely heard above the drumming of the meteorites.

I can't form words to answer her, the bijass is too close, so I hiss. There is no shelter to be had. This is all I can do. The best I can give her.

I don't know how much longer it lasts. It may have ended sooner or later than I know as I struggle for control but eventually the bijass retreats and I'm aware that it's over. Maeve's soft fingers are caressing my chest.

"It's over," she says. "Padraig, it's over."

Her voice pushes the last of the fog away. When I rise to my feet, I pull her up with me.

The landscape is dotted with new craters. Scanning, I assess for any further threats. All of that noise and vibration could attract the zemlja back. I kneel to place my palm against the ground, close my eyes, and wait. Maeve, brilliant as she is, stands silent. She doesn't question what I am doing, for which I'm most grateful and impressed.

There are no tremors. Nodding I rise again and meet her eyes.

"You're hurt," she gasps.

The pain is distant. I hardly feel it at all. She is okay and that is all that matters. As her hands reach towards me, she wavers and stumbles.

"Oh!" She cries out, looking down at her side.

Blood drips to the sand. She looks back at me, eyes wide, then collapses. I catch her before she hits the ground, and I lift her close to my chest but when I hold her close, pain stabs through my hearts. When I look at my torso, there's a piece of meteorite glass, embedded in my chest, appearing to have melded with my scales. It's painful, glinting in the sun.

"You're hurt," I say, focusing on her.

"So are you," she says, her face paler than normal.

"I'm fine," I say. "Let me attend your wound."

She opens her mouth, but snaps it shut without saying a word, then nods. Gently I lie her down close to the cliff face. Hesitantly, watching her eyes, I touch her shirt, then pull it up so I can see the wound. There's a good-sized cut covered in blood and several burns where hot shards hit her skin.

I get cloth and healing salve out of my pack. I pour some water over a piece of the cloth, then carefully touch it to her side. She jumps when it makes contact with her skin, gritting her teeth but not crying out.

Her eyes lock on mine and she nods, biting her lip.

Resuming the cleaning, I wash away the blood until I can see the wound itself. It's not as bad as it looked at first. When I touch it on either side, more blood pours out, and only then do I notice a piece of glass is embedded deep into her side.

"OW!" she cries out as I touch the glass. Darker blood wells up in the wound when she shifts.

"Be still," I say.

"You be still, that hurt!"

"I know, I am sorry, this will not be pleasant," I tell her.

Placing two fingers on either side of the wound I reach for the glass with my free hand. My fingers close on it, gripping.

A shocking pulse runs from my fingers to my hearts then down to my core. My first cock rages into a throbbing erection as overwhelming desire takes me.

He's so sexy. I want him.

Hearts pounding, blood rushing in my ears, cock throbbing, I stare at her all but panting. I've never felt anything like this. That thought, it wasn't mine.

Maeve's eyes are locked onto mine. Her eyelids are half-closed, her lips barely parted, a hint of her soft pink tongue showing. She's breathing heavily and then I feel her heart beat in my head, racing at a full gallop.

I let go of the glass, and it's gone. The connection broken. Silent, we watch each other.

"Padraig," she whispers.

Shaking my head, I don't have words to answer. This is more than I can handle. She needs medical attention from someone who understands human anatomy.

"We must go to the City," I say.

"You're hurt. It's too far," she says.

"I am fine," I say, smearing salve around the wound while I carefully avoid touching the glass. It slows the bleeding.

"No," she says, shaking her head. "You're not. Don't be a damn fool man, not now."

Confused, I stare at her, trying to decipher what she means.

"I am a male; how can I be else?" I ask.

Maeve rolls her eyes, pushes my hand away from her side, and pulls her shirt back into place. After sitting up slowly, she takes several deep breaths, then nods.

"Don't be dense," she mutters. "Turn around."

Unwilling to argue with her further, both because I'll probably lose, and because I don't understand what she's saying, I do as she says.

Her fingers touch the various wounds and she makes a tsk'ing sound. Suddenly I'm blinded by white-hot pain. Hissing I fight with the bijass that grabs for control.

"Oh, Padraig," she says, her voice soft.

"What is it?" I ask.

"You have pieces of glass embedded in your scales," she says. "And your wing…"

Straining to look over my shoulder I can't see what she's

31

talking about. My left wing has many holes through the membrane, which will slow me down in travelling.

"Okay," I say.

"Okay?" she asks, arching an eyebrow. "You've got pieces of glass melded into your scales, your wing is poked full of holes and all you say is okay?"

"Yes," I answer.

It's a reasonable response, what would she have me do?

"You're impossible," she sighs.

No words come to mind to answer her, so I say nothing. I'm not sure how it is impossible that I would be accepting of what is. There is nothing I can do to change the situation. She tends to my wounds with salve.

When she's done, she closes the small container and puts it away. She sits and leans her back against the cliff face, hanging her head down, her knees pulled up to her chest.

"We're a mess," she says.

"We're fine," I say. "I'll get you to the City."

"On that wing?" she asks, nodding towards my injury.

"Yes," I say, confident. "I will not fail you."

She sighs, shakes her head, then rises to her feet.

"Right," she says. "Let's do this."

Standing next to her a great sense of pride fills me. I am impressed with her grit and strength. If she would only be accepting, she would be an incredible mate. That familiar tightness in my core and sense of protectiveness pulses. I know, very well, she's the one.

We head for the City. Our travel is slow and difficult. My wing gives me more trouble than I want to admit. At times I carry her until she insists she can walk, and I let her while she can. The suns are setting and the first cries of sismis drift through the air by the time we approach the airlock to the City.

As we pass through the airlock some people help us and we're taken to the medical facilities they have here.

"What happened?" the auburn-haired female called Lana asks as we are rushed past her.

"Meteorite shower," Maeve answers.

"Oh," she says, both hands covering her swollen belly.

An image of Maeve with her belly swollen with our child flashes in my thoughts. A future that will never be, but my inner dragon doesn't care, it wants what it wants. Faintly I hear her heartbeat in my head, and the moment of touching the glass embedded in her side rises in my thoughts. She's my treasure, no matter how I fight it.

Lana stays behind as we go into the medical center. Inside we're separated and taken to different rooms.

As the humans take her away, my gaze lingers, and she keeps looking at me. As she passes through a door, she mouths a thank you.

I let the other humans lead me to where they tend my wounds. My thoughts stay with Maeve while they poke and prod, circling around the connection I felt to her when I touched the glass.

"Some of this we won't be able to remove," a human male says, peering closely at the wounds. "You're going to have new décor to show off."

"It is fine," I say, shaking my head.

I don't know this male and his words are insufficient to pull me out of my thoughts. Something is different even if I can't quite ascertain what it is. My hearts beat, steady and even, but I'm strangely aware of them. Concentrating on them there is a hint of an echo. It's not something I hear, really, any more than I hear my own hearts beating normally but it's definitely there.

I'm jerked out of my thoughts by a sudden sharp and stabbing pain.

"Hiss-sss," comes out of my mouth.

"Sorry," the male says. "That one is particularly deep."

He's poking at the large piece of shiny black meteorite in my chest. Staring at it I see my own reflection but mirrored over it I see Maeve. Ridiculous. How can this even be?

"Are you almost finished?" I ask. "I am due for patrol at the Village."

"Sure," he says. "There's not much I can do for you as it is. Your wing will heal but won't be of much use for a week at least. The rest of your body is already adjusting—most of the pieces look like they will push out on their own. The only one I'm concerned about is this one in your chest."

He stares at it with tight lips and his brow furrowed.

"It will be fine," I say.

"Right," he says, shaking his head. "Let me see you again in about a week. We should keep an eye on that."

"Fine," I agree, not really caring.

I don't need a human poking at me. My body is my tool, it will do as I tell it. Standing I walk out of the room and look in either direction down the empty hall. There is no sign or indication where they took Maeve.

The last I saw of her they were heading down my left, so I turn that way. Listening for sounds, I finally overhear voices and pick up my pace.

"You need to rest," a female voice says. "We can't take that piece out. I can cut it down, but I'm afraid if we remove it, we'll cause more damage than leaving it."

"Great," Maeve's voice says. "Well, I don't have time to rest. I have duties back with the Tribe. Patch me up, and I'll be on my way."

My chest swells, and I smile so broad it hurts my cheeks. That is a female worthy of any male's attention. Strong, vibrant and independent. What more could any male ask for in a mate?

I start through the door then think better of it. She's commented many times that I am rude. I should heed her words. Pausing, I knock on the wall, announcing my presence.

The door swings open and a female stands there, a hand on her hip, sharp eyes staring me down.

"Calista," I greet her. "I would see Maeve."

"You would, would you?" Calista asks. She looks over her shoulder, and Maeve must give some sign of assent as Calista moves to one side, letting me pass.

Maeve sits on a bed dressed in a loose white gown. The blood is cleaned up, and while she still seems paler than normal, she is very much alive and vibrant. A low, electric buzz passes across my scales, tingling as it goes.

"I'm fine," Maeve assures me, answering the unspoken question.

"Good," I respond, my eyes roaming over her.

She is perfect. Beautiful in more ways than I have words to express.

"You should rest," I say. "I have patrol duty at the village. I will come back here and get you after, then take you back to the Tribe."

Maeve arches an eyebrow, defiance flashing across her face in an instant.

"You will not 'come get me' like I'm some broken doll that needs looking after. I'm perfectly capable of traveling there on my own."

"It is not safe," I argue. "You're injured."

"And?" she asks, defiant, glaring with pursed lips.

I want to kiss those lips until they soften under my ministrations and welcome me. My mouth tingles, an itch crawls across my scales, and for an instant it's as if I can taste her on my tongue.

"And?" I ask, not understanding her point, ignoring the strange sensations.

"Exactly," she says, apparently winning an argument I don't understand.

My frown deepens as I grow irritated. Why can this female not let a male be a male? I am a protector! I would treasure her, she would want for nothing and never fear, but she will not accept me.

"Okay," I say, resigning myself and turning away.

"Padraig?" she says my name but it's a question more than a statement.

"Yes?" I ask over my shoulder, avoiding her gaze.

"Thank you," she says, a rare moment of gratitude in her voice.

"Of course," I answer, leaving the room, but as I do, hope blooms like the delicate leaves of a cvet.

3

MAEVE

"He likes you," Calista says, leaning against the wall with one foot propped up behind her.

"No, he doesn't," I say, shaking my head. "Ow!"

"Sorry," Addison says, looking up from her work. "You've got some nasty burns. I have to clean the dirt, sand, and pieces of glass out."

Tears sit in the corner of my eyes, but I refuse to shed them. If for no other reason than I don't want to let the pain win.

"Great," I say, gritting my teeth. "Let's get that over with."

Addison smiles and resumes cleaning the burns.

"He does," Calista continues, "trust me, I know."

Keeping my eyes closed against the pain, I contemplate her words. Maybe.

When he touched the piece of glass in my side... I've never felt anything like that. Desire, sure, but it was... too intense. Desire isn't a strong enough word for what I felt, but more than that, I swear I could sense his thoughts, feel his desire for me too.

Biting my lip, I shake my head again. "It's ridiculous."

"Okay," Calista says, crossing her arms over her chest, a wide grin across her face.

"You're impossible," I say through teeth gritted in pain.

"Sure," Callista says. "I pretty much thought that too, when I met Ladon. Look at us now."

"Ladon is nice, pleasant, easy to be around. Padraig is rough, abrasive, demanding, and overbearing."

"Ha!" Calista laughs. "You don't know Ladon! You should have seen him when Sverre first arrived. You would have thought the same thing or worse."

"You're kidding," I say.

"I've heard stories, she's not," Addison adds.

"But he's not like that now," I say.

"He's not as *much* like that now," Calista says. "I've been a good influence on him."

My body hurts, throbbing in areas, aching in others, burning in yet others. It's not making it easy to be in a good mood, and I certainly don't have enough left over to consider Padraig in a new light.

"Well, maybe," I say, pushing it aside for now.

"Think about it," Calista says.

"Sure," I agree, wincing again under Addison's ministrations. "The idea has come up about doing Christmas."

I throw that out there desperately wanting to change the subject. Something light and airy is exactly what I need right now. Anything to keep my mind off how badly I hurt.

"Seriously?" both of the women say as one.

"Yeah?" I look at both of them, confused by the immediate reaction. They look at each other, and I bounce my gaze back and forth between them. "What's the big deal?"

Calista shakes her head, mouth open, eyes wide. Addison frowns, then shrugs.

"Nothing," Addison says.

"I hadn't even thought of it," Calista says, pushing herself off the wall. "How crazy is that? We've been here how long and not one of us thought of doing Christmas."

"Well, we've all been busy with little things like surviving," I say.

"True," Calista says. "Can you imagine Illadon though? The look on his face when he sees presents for the first time? We haven't even had a proper birthday celebration for my little man."

The nostalgia is thick in her voice, her eyes are wet, and she wipes them quickly.

"So you both like the idea?" I ask.

"I love it," Calista says.

Addison doesn't say anything. Looking over my shoulder at her where she is working on my burns she's focused intently.

"Addison?" I ask.

"Yeah?" she asks, distractedly.

"You like the idea?" I repeat.

"Sure," she says, not looking away from the work but it's a half-hearted agreement at best.

Calista places a hand on my arm pulling my attention back to her. She shakes her head, lips pursed, and I let it drop though my curiosity burns as deep as the wounds on my backside.

"We'll work it out," Calista says. "I know Rosalind will support it. Anything that ties the three groups together she's going to love."

"Yeah," I agree.

Rosalind and Visidion are both always looking to strengthen the ties between the three disparate groups forming on Tajss. It's probably a good idea too. Earth history was a required class on the ship. All of us are familiar with the territory wars that plagued humanity for generations. When there were small, idealistic countries that would go to war with each other over a clash of ideas or control of a piece of land.

I hadn't thought about it much, but it's definitely something that could happen here on Tajss. The Tribe, the City, and the Village each have access to different resources that the others need. As long as we keep open trade and support, we'll be fine. I've also heard the stories about how the Village came to be, the Gershom coup and the results of that.

I don't envy our leaders their work.

"Okay," Addison says. "Now we're down to this, roll onto your side."

Obediently I lie down on my side, gritting my teeth as she probes at the piece of meteorite stuck into my other side. Calista comes forward and holds my hand. I try not to squeeze hers too hard, but every time Addison touches around the wound, pain shoots up my side and explodes in my head. Tears flow freely but I proudly don't cry out.

"Well..." Addison says, trailing off.

"Well?" I ask, not liking the tone of her voice in the least. Addison and Calista exchange a look, but I can't read the meaning of it. "Tell me."

Addison helps me over to a sitting position. She purses her lips, staring at the bed while taking off the latex gloves. The gloves snap as she removes them, walks to a bin and drops them in. The silence is heavy, laden with bad news that no one wants to say and I'm not sure I want to hear. Cold sweat drips down my back as I brace myself for the worst.

"I can't take it out," she says, finally.

"Okay..." I say, letting it trail off.

"Somehow it didn't hit anything major. Your liver was nicked, but that will heal fine with the antibiotics and other meds I've given you."

"And?" I ask.

"One, it's going to hurt, quite a bit, for a while," she says.

"And?" I ask, again.

She shakes her head and sighs. "And I don't know. It could be nothing, it could be something. Physically there's nothing that badly wrong. It's embedded into you in a way that I can't remove because it's—"

She stops midsentence, meeting my eyes for the first time. She squares her shoulders, inhales deeply, then gives me a half smile.

"Addison, you're scaring me," I admit.

"I'm sorry, that's not my intention," she says. "I've never seen or even heard of anything like this. It's melded with your skin and as near as I can see with your ribs as well. It's a part of you. If I try to remove it now, it will cause a shock to your system that I don't believe you'll survive."

"Oh," I say, the weight of her words hitting me and stealing my breath.

"But you'll be fine," Calista says, her voice insistent. "Right Addison?"

"Yes," Addison says. "I believe so."

"You believe?" I ask, my voice cracking at the end.

"Addison," Calista admonishes.

"Right. You will be, of course."

"What is it you're not telling me?" I ask. Addison and Calista share another look. "Tell me."

"You know the meteorite glass has properties that we're still studying," Addison says. "It puts off energy field we don't understand. It's beyond our comprehension right now and I don't honestly know what the effect could be on our bodies in handling it, much less having a good size piece melded into your skin and ribs."

"I see," I say, nodding and biting my lip.

"It's probably nothing," Addison says.

My thoughts return to the sensation and the connection that happened right after between Padraig and myself. As soon as they do, something shifts. My heart beats loud in my head, but it has a strange double echo to it. My skin warms and it's as if a warm breeze blows across me.

"Maeve?" Calista asks, staring.

"Yeah?" I ask, shaking my head to clear it yet still I hear that echo of my heartbeat.

"What's happening?" Addison asks, placing a hand on my forehead.

"Nothing," I lie.

I don't know why I don't want to talk about this. The denial slipped out before I had time to think of it. Somehow it feels right. I don't know what this is, but I do know that I'm done with being poked and prodded.

"Maeve," Calista takes both of my hands and her eyes bore into mine. "We're here for you."

Smiling I nod and squeeze her hands. "Thank you. Really, I'm fine."

"Good," Calista says.

"You should rest," Addison says. "A few days bedrest would be best."

"I'm not staying here that long," I say. "I'll go back to the Tribe tomorrow."

"That's not a good idea," Addison says.

"It's what's going to happen," I insist. "I'm fine. I have duties—I can't dump them all."

"You need to rest," Addison insists.

"Right," I agree. "I'll do that after I do my duties."

"I think some of the men are going to journey to the Tribe for a food exchange," Calista says. "She could go with them."

"I don't like it," Addison says, but I can hear her conviction wavering in her voice.

"I promise to not overdo it, but if I don't get back, they'll be worried. I do have duties, but I can trade around for some lighter ones, I'm sure."

"No lifting, no exertion, not for at least a week," Addison says.

"Got it," I agree.

"Fine," she says. "But don't you tear up my good work, you hear? Those are some very nice stitches."

"You got it," I grin.

4

PADRAIG

*T*he cries of the sismis hunting echo through the night. They're of no concern as I continue my patrol around the Village. I'm barely aware of them. My thoughts are consumed with her.

Something has changed. Exactly what that change is and what it means is not clear. On one hand, there is my innate, bodily desire, born in every Zmaj male, something I'm trying to deny due to her apparent lack of interest, but it's more than that. I think, or I hope. That is the question, is it real? Or am I projecting my primal instinct and desire to have her as my treasure into an unwelcome advance?

I would never force her into anything, of course. No matter how I hate to admit it, she is my treasure. No male would treat his treasure in such a way. That would be inconceivable. So, is this real? What is it, exactly, that changed?

When we touched, that's the moment everything shifted. After the meteorite shower, the look on her face convinced me that she felt it too. That moment replays in my mind's eye as I walk a wide perimeter around the Village.

Below the images is her heartbeat, echoing behind my

own hearts beating. Soft, subtle, but definitively there. It's a feeling or an awareness or... something. It's new, different, and I wonder, does she feel it too? Is she as aware of me as I am of her? Does she welcome it?

I've never heard of such a thing, which makes me doubt all of it. I worry I'm fooling myself out of thwarted desire. I've never been one for self-deception. I know who and what I am and have no doubts on my own shortcomings and strengths. The bijass though, it is a strange thing. Could it be subtly driving me towards my more primal instincts?

Once, in dim tales from before our civilization, it was told in ancient stories that the Zmaj culture was different. Everything from before the Devastation is a dim memory now and those stories are even more remote, something I barely have fragments of from when I was a child being educated for my role in society.

Tales of violent males who took what they wanted and refused to be tamed. Sometimes they were told as epic tales of heroism, but most were cautionary tales of who and what we could become, if we didn't hold to the ideals. If we let our darker, primal instincts come to the forefront.

Something I've been accused of more than once, even among the Tribe. The Edicts help, but still, the rage boils inside me, red, hot, ready to spill over into action at the blink of an eye. Violent, wrong action usually, but action nonetheless.

"Maeve," I say to the empty dark.

Her name is sweetness on my tongue as it rolls off, drifting into the night. Something pulses in my chest and a cold chill runs across my scales. My wings rustle and I shiver in reaction. At the same time, I sense her, an awareness I can't explain—but I know, with absolute certainty, that she's sleeping. Dreaming, as my attention drifts to her across the space separating us. She is warm and safe.

Happiness wells in my core and spreads out across my body. I can't recall ever having such a sensation. It takes me a few minutes to figure out what to even call it. Maybe, before the Devastation, before I was trapped in that mine and left to die, before all of this I might have known it. Maybe.

I don't recall it if I did.

And it doesn't matter. She's the source. She is everything.

A hiss escalates into a high-pitched howl as something slams into my side. I'm knocked to the ground, struggling to grab onto my attacker. Razor-sharp teeth snap just over my face, and foul breath assaults my nostrils as it tries to clamp down.

I can't find a grip on the thing's leathery skin. I'm disoriented, my breath knocked out by the impact, I punch with every ounce of strength I can. My fist slams into the side of its head, then slides up, making contact with a sharp spine that slides along my protective scales.

Only then does it click what is on me. A guster. One of the most dangerous predators on the planet, and I let it get the jump on me.

Slamming my tail into its side, I keep punching the side of its head. I have to get it off. If I slip and it gets its teeth into me it's over. It hisses loudly when my tail makes contact, but searing pain blinds me at the same time. Some of its spines pierce my scales, finding flesh. Jerking my tail back is almost as bad, as the spines break, sticking in my flesh.

Red rage floods in behind the pain, and the bijass takes over. Hissing loudly, I grab its jaws with both hands as it drives in, trying to clamp down on me again. Its sharp teeth cut into the flesh of my fingers, but the bijass doesn't allow for pain.

Shifting my grip, I hold its mouth open, forcing it wider. The guster hisses, a gurgling edge to it, as I force it open wider. It's feet scramble on either side of me, pulling back,

46

giving me space. Rising with it as it pulls back, I keep my grip, mostly because its teeth have pierced my flesh, making my grip for me.

"Padraig!" a voice calls, distant, coming from the far side of the rage.

This monster dies. Shred it, dominate it, it's mine.

Rational thoughts barely form through the heavy fog of the bijass. Other Zmaj arrive, but I'm dimly aware of them. The thing in my hands is what matters, and it must pay for having caused me pain. It must know I am its master.

Roaring I pull, pouring all I have into it. A loud snapping sound, and then it goes limp, dropping to the ground. After dropping it, I spread my arms and wings wide, kicking it in the head as I roar my victory. I turn away from my kill and look for the next opponent.

The other Zmaj are engaged already. More guster, a pack then. Good. More to destroy.

A sensation cuts through the rage. My brothers. I'm aware of them, suddenly, in a new and different way. Arawn laughs as his lochaber flashes in the air over his head, spinning gracefully as he parries the guster he faces. Darting in and out with fast feints, dodges, and attacks.

Bashir is fighting to my left. I'm aware of both males, connected with them, and it's strange as it pushes aside the bijass. These are my brothers.

The two males finish the guster they are fighting quickly. A female and offspring it would seem. Scanning the night carefully but finding no other threats I face my fellows.

"Thank you," I say, a sense of gratefulness and belonging swells my chest.

"Of course," Arawn says, holding out his hand.

Looking at his extended hand, impulsively, I take it then pull him close, slamming our chests together and I pat his back.

"Wow," Bashir says, looking down at the guster I dispatched. "You don't mess around, do you?"

The broken creature lies on the ground before us.

"We can harvest this meat," Arawn says, stepping back from my embrace, a strange look on his face.

"Right," I agree.

It's a good idea, of course. The look on his face is enigmatic, thoughtful. I understand because I'm not sure what I'm doing either. What is this feeling?

The three of us set about the job of harvesting. Silence reigns as we work. It gives me time to think, which I'm glad to have.

My thoughts spin around in ridiculous circles and behind them I'm still aware of that faint heartbeat. There is no doubt any longer, the beat is Maeve's heart.

Somehow, we're connected. Perhaps there is some property to the meteorite shards. Maybe it's fate. I know she is the one my inner fire has selected. She is my perfect mate, or will be, at some point, I hope.

Mates don't always work out. I remember this from before. Sometimes fate has new twists, or something happens to one or the other. It wasn't common, but it did happen often enough to be talked about.

None of us talk about that though. We don't talk at all. Perhaps it's a male thing. Are we avoiding looking at a harsh truth? There are only a handful of males who aren't bonded. Is there something to that?

The humans outnumber us. There are many potential females. How is it that those of us without bond are not yet mated?

Out of the corner of my eye, I notice Arawn watching me when he thinks I'm not looking. Curiosity colors his scales. Strangely, I feel a connection to him as well. A sense of brotherhood.

Dimly I recall having such a feeling, but it was from long before the Devastation. The distant memories are better off forgotten. I don't want them or need them.

They fly out of the fog of the bijass despite my desire to not remember them. I don't recall them exactly, they're single moments, broken up, disjointed, leaving me with only the cold certainty that I was left for dead by those I trusted.

Abandoned.

Cold settles in my chest. The connection that I was feeling to my brothers in arms cools, returning to normal. We finish the harvesting of the meat, but it's now close to morning. The first hints of the dawn light the distant horizon.

"That is that," Arawn says, his eyes watching, missing nothing.

"Right," I agree. "Will you take this haul back to the Village?"

I direct my question at Bashir.

"Yes," he says.

"What are you going to do?" Arawn asks.

"I'm going to make another circuit before calling it for the night," I say.

"Okay," he says, curiosity in his voice but he doesn't say more, walking off with Bashir.

Watching them walk away, the sensation of belonging remains. Shaking my head, I turn from their retreating forms and walk. This is a new and different feeling and I'm not sure what to think of it.

The suns slowly rise above the horizon, rays of light like stretching fingers crawling across the sand. Stopping I watch the shadows being chased away. A quiet settles across my thoughts.

The only thing I can compare it with is when I'm working the forge. When the world becomes the piece of metal I'm shaping. I see what that piece can be, and I work it towards that. It's a combination of imposing my will, but also of working with what is there.

Somehow this feels similar. A new path ahead, one I'm forging. One, I hope, that Maeve is going to walk with me. The only question in my mind is how do I convince her this is the path we should be walking? Will she see it as well? Can she agree, become malleable like steel softened in the heat of the forge. Strong, yet workable?

This will be the greatest challenge I will face. I like a challenge.

Smiling, I set off to finish my patrol.

5

MAEVE

"*F*inally, home," I say, unable to stop the grin spreading across my face.

It's strange how much I miss this place. I haven't been here with the Tribe that long, but it's home to me now. There's a strong connection for me to this place. Stronger than I think I realized I had.

"Happy?" Ladon asks.

"Yes," I say, nodding enthusiastically. "Thanks for the escort."

"Of course," he says.

As we approach the gate in the wall, it swings open and we're welcomed inside. The moment we walk through, I see Delilah running out of the main cave.

For politeness' sake, I glance at Ladon, but I barely wait for his nod before I run to meet my dear friend. We crash into each other, embracing one another. She plants kisses on each of my cheeks before pushing back and holding me by the shoulders.

"Are you crazy!" she exclaims.

"Maybe?" I laugh.

"I've been worried sick about you," she says.

"I sent a message," I protest.

"A message isn't good enough," she says, shaking her head. "I missed you, girl."

"I missed you, too," I say, laughing. "But it's only been a few days."

"Sure, sure," she waves my answer away. "Days that seemed like months, at least."

Warmth fills my core. It's good to have friends and to have been missed. When I inhale deeply, even the air seems fresher now that I'm back where I feel like I belong. Looking around, turning a slow circle, everything feels fresh, new, as if I haven't really seen it before.

My eyes stop on the workshop area when I see Padraig. Instantly that faint double beat echoes my heartbeat in my head. It's strange as if I feel what he's feeling in some way. He's staring in my direction, the heavy blacksmith's hammer of his work stopped mid-swing.

I may not say it out loud, especially where he could hear it, but damn he looks good. That pose makes all of his muscles bulge and stand out in strained relief. A shiver runs down my spine, and my lower stomach tightens and knots.

Wow.

"Yeah, he missed you too," Delilah says, a teasing note to her voice.

"No way," I say, shaking my head.

"Oh yes, way," she answers. "Every day he's asking after you. I don't know how many times the other men have had to work to make him stay here and not go to the City. He's needed right now, or I'm sure he'd have been gone."

"I'm sure it's nothing," I say, unable to take my eyes off of him.

"Right," she says, and I see, out of the corner of my eye her looking between him and me. "He's different too. What happened out there?"

"It was, well, scary," I admit.

"Sure, come on now, tell me all the details. I want the juicy bits!"

Laughing, I turn towards her, tearing my eyes off of Padraig. It doesn't help, really. I feel his eyes burning into my back, his heartbeats in my head, and there's a desire that is not entirely mine. My cheeks flush hot. I have to get those thoughts out of my head!

"Let's get to work," I say. "I'll tell you all about it while we do."

"Deal," Delilah says.

Together we walk across the open area and past the flourishing garden. Several women are working the rows of plants, weeding, harvesting, cleaning out the irrigation channels. All the daily duties that make it all work.

They're distant in my thoughts though. I may have looked away, but the majority of my attention is on Padraig. This is ridiculous. He's not the man for me. Rude, abrasive, domineering—if he was human, I'd file him as a chauvinist, but I'm not sure that applies to an alien-dragon like him.

Oh what the heck, it does. He's like... what? Captain Kirk on steroids? Fight it rather than think it through?

That's kind of a good analogy. Comparing Kirk to Picard. Kirk was always about the brawn while Picard would think things through.

Nodding to myself in satisfaction I grab up a box of vegetables and work to prep them for storage.

"Details, girl," Delilah prods.

I check to make sure we're alone in the prep area, which makes it easier for me to share. Though I don't know how much to tell. It's strange, and I'm not sure a lot of it is even real. Maybe I'm projecting or imagining the connection to him.

"The meteorite storm took us by surprise. I was hit with a few shards and one embedded into me."

"You're kidding!" Delilah exclaims.

"No," I say, shaking my head.

Pausing my work, I pull the side of my shirt up to reveal the piece of meteorite glass that is embedded into my side. It sparkles in the candle's light.

Delilah gasps, leaning in close, one hand hovering over it, obviously afraid to touch it without asking.

"Go ahead," I say.

"Does it hurt?" she asks.

"Some, yeah," I say. "It's not awful though. Addison cut it down, so it doesn't protrude as much."

"Why didn't she take it out?"

"Apparently it's melded to my ribs, or something like that."

"Wow," she says, delicately touching it.

The piece of glass flashes. It's easy to see in the dim light inside the cave. Delilah jerks her hand back, and I gasp as an electric tingle races through my limbs.

"Woah," I exclaim.

"Are you okay?" she asks, worried.

"Yeah," I say, shaking my head. "I haven't seen it do that before."

"This is so strange," she says. "This planet, that, everything."

"You're telling me," I agree.

"Okay, well, let's leave that alone," she says, decisively. "Tell me the rest. All of it, don't leave out a single, juicy detail."

Smiling, I grab up a root vegetable and my knife.

"What do you want to know?" I ask, knowing very well what she wants.

"How was he? Did he save you? Was it heroic? Come on, you know what I want!"

"Yeah, I guess it was pretty heroic."

"He has glass embedded into his scales too," she says. "And his one wing looks like it took a hell of a beating."

"He protected me," I say.

"Oh! More!"

I launch into the details of my adventure, but I carefully leave out any mention of what happened when we touched after the glass was embedded into us. It's not that I don't trust her, I do, implicitly. It's more that I don't understand it, and I'm still not sure it's even real. How can it be?

Of course, as I think that, I hear his hearts beating in my head. I've decided that's what it has to be. What else could it be? Outside the I'm Crazy Option, there's always that one, I suppose.

Would it be strange to go crazy? Looking at my life the past few years going off my rocker seems a reasonable response. Crash landing on this desert planet, rescued by one alien-dragon, finding an entire village of alien-dragons.

Yup, none of that seems crazy, does it? Oh and our two, completely different species happen to also be biologically compatible. Let's not forget that piece of the puzzle. Also, that there are no Zmaj women. None, so we're the answer to their prayers or whatever they do along the same lines.

Or... maybe... I'm in a padded cell on the ship. None of this is anything more than my own delusional ravings. It's all a bad fever dream or part of my psychotic break.

No, I'm not that creative.

"Well, I can tell you," Delilah says after I finish my tale. "Padraig is different."

"He is?" I ask, a deeper and stronger curiosity in my guts than I want to admit to.

"Definitely," she says, nodding to accent the word. "He hasn't been in a single fight since he got back from the Village."

"Really?" I ask, mouth dropping open in surprise.

"Nope, not a single one. He even said something nice to Samil."

"You are kidding me!" I exclaim.

"If only, I swear when it happened everyone in a hundred yards stopped and stared."

"I bet!"

"So, something happened," she probes.

"Yeah, well beats me what," I lie because I feel him in the back of my head.

He's changing. Does that mean I am too? Is this connection between us real? Am I imagining it? Too many questions and I don't have any answers.

Delilah stares at me, waiting for me to say something, anything, but I don't have any more to offer. I turning to her to offer a smile and then a shrug. Her stare lingers.

"Okay," she says, at last. "If that's the way it is."

"It's nothing to do with what it 'is'," I say, annoyance rising. "It's all there is."

"Sure," she says, smiling broader. "There's also nothing between the two of you, nothing to see here, move along."

"You're impossible," I say, unable to keep myself from laughing at her jibes.

"Just wait, I get better," she quips.

"Great, I can't wait to see it," I reply.

We turn and walk towards the main cave and our duties. Olivia and Ragnar are coming our way with their daughter.

"Hey," I say, waving my fingers at Zoe.

Zoe sits on her mother's hip, almost too big to be carried

that way any longer. She's growing fast on top of already being a big girl when she was born. All the Zmaj-human babies are big for their age.

Zoe waggles her fingers at me, her bright eyes sparkling. Olivia pauses, shifting Zoe's weight. She has to lean to one side to keep her up.

"What are you all doing?" Delilah asks.

"We have to go to the City," she huffs. "Addison wants to do checkups on all the babies."

"Oh, sounds fun," I say.

Olivia rolls her eyes. "If that's what you want to call it."

"It is sensible," Ragnar says, placing a protective hand on Olivia's back.

"I know, but I don't have time for this! Our meat stores are barely sufficient to last a month and now we're having to send supplies to help the Village plus trade with the City. We should be here."

"Yes, my love," Ragnar says, a broad smile on his face.

"Daddy!" Zoe exclaims, reaching her hands out to him.

Ragnar's face lights up when his daughter reaches for him. He sweeps her off her mother's hip, lifting her high into the air. Zoe screams in delight, her tiny wings flapping in the air and her tail buzzing with excitement.

"Daddy!" she peals laughter out, and my heart swells watching them.

Ragnar tosses her gently up into the air, catching her on the descent then tossing her up again. Olivia watches with pure joy on her face. The love between the three of them is palpable, a thick blanket laid over all of us in this shared moment of family.

"I think we have a crate of supplies to go, can you guys take them along?" Delilah asks.

"We're going alone, it would be difficult to carry," Ragnar says, barely taking his attention off Zoe.

"I can go along," I offer. "If you don't mind."

"Go along where?" a deep bass voice inserts itself into our conversation.

Before I look, I know who it is. His presence fills me, consuming my attention. My breath catches and my heart leaps into my throat. A strange, pulsing sensation emanates from the glass in my side.

Padraig.

"To the City," I say, turning towards him.

"Oh," he says, his voice soft.

Has his deep, rumbling voice always sounded so silky smooth? It's almost like it caresses my skin.

"Would you like to come?" Ragnar asks.

"No, I have duties here," Padraig, says not taking his eyes off of me.

"Okay," Ragnar says, either oblivious or deliberately ignoring the tension in the air. "Duty first."

"Go, go, go!" Zoe says, bouncing in her Daddy's arms and pointing.

"Yes, love," Ragnar says. "Soon."

"I'll get that box," Delilah says, but I see her eyes going between Padraig and me.

Thanks Delilah, call attention to the awkwardness, why don't you?

"Well, I should go help her," I say, latching on to a way out of whatever this is.

I can't name it, but it's not comfortable at all. I don't know what to say or how to act. In my head, his heartbeat pounds behind every thought, calling to me almost. It's more than that too, he doesn't want me to go, I sense that.

Why?

What are we to each other? Is there something here?

No. No way. He's not my type, not the one for me. Steeling my resolve, I give him a curt nod and walk away. The entire way though, I feel his gaze burning into my back. I do not add any sway to my hips, nope, not a bit.

"I'm so glad you came," Calista says. "An extra set of hands is always needed. How are you feeling?"

She glances at my side when she asks, not mentioning the glass embedded into me while clearly inquiring about it. I appreciate her discretion though I don't think it's overly necessary.

"Good," I say. "It's not bad at all really. Mostly I can forget it's there."

"What's where?" Jolie asks, curiously.

I pull up my shirt exposing the glass embedded into my side.

"OH!" Jolie exclaims, her almond-shaped eyes widening.

She leans in close to inspect it.

"I thought all the pieces were removed," she says, straightening.

Dropping my shirt back into place I shake my head.

"That one was too embedded," I say.

"Mommy!" Rverre shouts, pulling all of our attention.

She has climbed on top of the cabinets that line the wall of the waiting area Addison has set up. Once she's assured all eyes are on her she smiles broadly, spreads her arms wide and leaps towards Jolie.

"Rverre!" Jolie yells, rushing to intercept her daughter but she's too late.

Rverre flies through the air with a surprising grace. Illadon shouts in pleasure, encouraging her and Rverre's laughter peals through the room.

Jolie reaches over her head trying to catch her but at the

last possible moment Rverre tilts to one side and flies sideways between her Mother's grasping hands.

"Rverre!" Jolie exclaims, frustration making her voice high-pitched.

""Mommy, I did it!" Rverre exclaims landing lightly behind Jolie, she turns and takes a bow.

"Well done," Illadon says, clapping.

"Don't do that!" Jolie says, shaking her head. "You could have been hurt."

"No, I couldn't," Rverre counters. "I have wings, see?"

She turns her back and flaps her delicate wings. Jolie scoops her up and snuggles her in her arms.

"Yes, dear, you do. That doesn't mean it's always safe. You could be hurt. Mommy worries."

"Don't worry Mommy, we're tough!" Rverre laughs and points at Illadon.

While all of us were watching Rverre he has climbed up to the top of the cabinets himself. He leaps as we turn, gliding a short distance, then somersaults midair, spreads his wings and hovers for a moment with his arms out wide.

"Whoo!" he shouts, tilts forward and glides a few more feet before landing.

"Oh!" Rverre exclaims. "My turn!"

"Enough," Calista says, kneeling before Illadon. "Do you want me to talk to your father about how you've been behaving?"

"No, Mommy," Illadon replies, completely unabashed, a devilish grin spreading across his face and delight dancing in his eyes.

"Okay, now be good," she says.

"This is boring!" he exclaims, stomping one bare foot.

His toes have small claws on them, like the Zmaj men. Illadon dresses like the Zmaj, shirtless, opting to wear only loose-fitting pants that tie at the waist. His scales sparkle in the flickering light of the room.

In his face I see Calista more than Ladon. He has her nose and the color of their eyes are similar. There's something to the structure of his cheeks and bone structure that puts me in mind of her too. The rest of him is pure Ladon. Despite his young age, he's brawny, muscles already forming giving him a lot of muscle definition.

Someday, maybe I could have a baby of my own. Warmth forms in my belly, slowly crawling out. It'd be nice, wouldn't it?

It's not like we're ever getting off this planet. On the ship I used to think about having a family one day. It was, after all, expected that all women would. It was part of the culture, what you did, more than anything, but I think it was also part of the initial plan. A generation ship wouldn't be much good if there weren't generations being born.

In the back of my head thrums that now familiar throbbing double beat. I immediately think of Padraig. An empty sensation swells that feels like I moved too fast. It makes me slightly light-headed. As I focus on the feeling the room tilts.

"You okay?" Jolie asks.

"Huh?" I ask, forcing myself to focus on my surroundings.

Jolie moves to me and takes my arms in her hands. She stares into my eyes, searching.

"What's happening? Is it the glass?" she asks.

Calista is next to her now, the two children taking the opportunity to scamper around the room chasing each other. The patter of their clawed feet on the tiled floor counteracts the beats thrumming in my head. It helps me to get out of my own head.

"No, it's... nothing," I say.

"Right," Calista says, pursing her lips. "You're seeing Addison next."

"I'm fine, seriously. This time is for the kids," I say.

"The kids are fine, this is only a checkup. She's monitoring their growth and development. If something is happening to you, that is what needs to be looked into," Jolie insists.

"You are both, wonderful," I smile. "It means a lot how easily you've welcomed me and all of us."

"There aren't that many of us left," Calista observes. "And we've seen the effects separatism and hate can have."

There's a dark tone to her last statement and I know she's referring to Gershom and his 'camp' of followers.

"Right," I smile. "But I'm fine, seriously. Maybe a bit of water, probably a little dehydrated. It's not like it's easy to stay hydrated here."

"You are taking epis, right?" Jolie asks, arching an eyebrow.

"Yeah," I answer.

"Good," she says. "There are a few who still refuse. I don't know what they're holding out for, but I wish they would realize we're here and this is it. We have to make—Rverre!"

Rverre laughs loudly as her mother calls her name. One of the stools that line the wall is burning brightly.

"Sorry mommy," she grins. "I burped."

Jolie and Calista work in unison to put out the small fire. I stare in shock.

"Uh," I say, mouth slack and unable to form a word out of the storm of thoughts racing in my head.

"It's nothing," Calista says. "They don't have full control of their glands yet."

"Their glands?" I ask.

"You know the Zmaj can breathe fire, right?" Jolie asks, not looking up from putting out the fire.

"Okay," I say, shaking my head.

The things I learn every day on this planet. Jolie laughs.

"Look at her face," she says.

"Surprise," Calista responds, laughing as well.

Maybe having a Zmaj baby wouldn't be such a great idea after all. It's not enough that you have to deal with all the normal aspects of a baby, but one that might accidentally set the house on fire?

It's so absurd I can't help but laugh with them.

"Next!" Addison calls, opening the door and looking out.

"Come on Illadon, that's us," Calista says, taking his hand and leading him through the door.

"Aww," he moans. "I don't want to. She's going to poke me, again."

"I know love," Calista says. "Remember, it's for your good. You're the first of your kind."

"And the best!" Illadon says, puffing out his chest.

"No, you're not!" Rverre yells at his retreating form. "Anything you can do, I can do better!"

"Bah!" Illadon exclaims. "Girls--"

The rest of his words are cut off by the closing of the door. It's so cute I could burst. It's clear how close the two children are, like their mothers.

That empty ache stays in the back of my thoughts, reminding me how nice it would be to have something more. That missing piece to life.

Sighing, I invite Rverre to play tic-tac-toe with me. She sits across from me and we begin the game.

6

PADRAIG

he heat of the forge radiates across my scales. Warm and welcoming. I pull the steel from it, lay it on my anvil, and strike it with my hammer, forcing it to bend to my will. Working steel is soothing. Natural. It makes sense.

Unlike her.

How can any female be the way she is? How can she not want a male to protect and provide for her? We are perfect for each other, if she would see it. The fact she doesn't baffles me.

My hammer clangs, over and over, and even the sound of it calms me. Predictable. The rhythm of it is easy to go with. It washes away all other concerns and problems.

The orange-red steel flattens, slowly taking on the shape I want it to have. It feels good. Creator, enforcer, it is what a male should be. It is what she should want in a male.

Except she doesn't.

Under the beating of the hammer against the anvil lies another thrumming, regular beat that echoes behind my thoughts. I try not to focus on it overmuch, but it's always there. Behind everything, calling to me. An awareness of her.

If I focus on it, then I feel her.

I should not have let her go alone. If I'd forced myself onto the journey though, it would have made her angry. I don't know why, but I know, with the same certainty I know it's her heart I hear in my head, that it would.

We've barely spoken since she returned from the City. When we meet, the connection between us throbs. I believe she feels it as well as I do, but she doesn't give me any indication of what she feels or thinks.

She is so... strange. Different. What do I make of this female? How do I make her mine?

There has to be a way for me to forge her, to show her what we could be together.

If she were metal, it would be a matter of finding the right temperature to make her malleable without breaking her.

That's important. I would never bring her harm, not in any way. I do not want to break her, I want her to accept me.

Interesting.

Is that the key? Am I the one who must change to fit her?

How do I change myself? I am who I am. I am a male. I cannot be other. Can I?

Bah, this is getting nowhere.

Resignation settles in, and I push aside all thoughts of Maeve. Losing myself in the forging and letting the world carry on without my attention to it.

"Padraig!" Samil yells to be heard over the clanging.

Stopping mid-swing, I glare at the smaller Zmaj. The tint of his scales shifts to show hints of fear, but the look in his eyes is steel.

"What?" I ask, surprisingly not feeling the anger I normally would at being interrupted during my work.

"Invaders!" he shouts, pointing at the wall.

Cold races across my scales. I drop the hammer and grab my lochaber where it leans against the cliff face, and I run.

The shouts echoing are clear now. I'd lost myself to my work and didn't hear them. Cursing myself, I tighten my grip on my weapon.

A zipping sound is followed by the sound of impact and a small explosion. Arawn, Melchior, and Ragnar are at the gate, running through it.

Spreading my wings, I leap and catch the soft air currents, gliding faster than I can run. When I land, I'm already running. The shouts of battle engaged reach my ears and along with cries of pain.

The bijass surges forward, red rage clouding my vision. No one will threaten me or mine.

Bursting through the open gate I pause for only a moment to take in the scene. Invaders.

We've fought them off before but there are a lot of them and they have their guns. Arawn and Melchior fight a group of four, Ragnar has three on his own. Samil skids to a stop next to me.

"Take that one," I order, pointing at a lone Invader.

"On it," he says, no hesitation.

He's growing, good. A sense of pride wells in my chest. Why am I proud of Samil? Strange.

A fresh group of invaders approaches. There are six of them, armed with guns, wearing their strange armor that leaves parts of their lithe, long bodies exposed to show their six arms, muscles and strange body art.

These are mine.

Roaring, I race at them. I leap into the air and whirl the lochaber over my head. After landing hard a few feet in front of the approaching group, I swing my weapon over and down, slicing the first of them across both his arms. Blood explodes into the air in red droplets, spattering across the sand.

The rest fire without bothering to aim. Fast shots, most of which go wide. Three of them engage with me, while the other three circle wide, working their way past me.

It's clear they don't want to fight me, so they must have another goal in mind. It doesn't matter what that goal is, I will stop them.

Using the staff of the lochaber on the backswing I force the three engaged with me, including the one I've already cut, to step back, giving me room.

I jump backwards, intercepting those trying to slip away. Crouching, I thrust the lochaber staff at one, feinting high, then reversing and stabbing the blunt end into the calf of his leg. A crack, and he collapses to the ground, one leg broken.

"Hold the line!" I yell. "They want the cave!"

Epis. What else could they want? If they were Zzlo, I would suspect them of wanting captives for their slave trade, but they are not those monsters.

Over the sounds of battle there comes a rumble. The ground shakes. I'm facing six enemies, and now something else comes too.

My lochaber moves through the air with blinding speed. Parry, thrust, block, keep moving. If I pause, they'll break past me.

As one they rush, surrounding me. Driving into the two closest to me I smash one in the face with a fist while using the lochaber to block the other's attack.

They're not using their weapons to best effect. Why?

Something pulses in my head and then it hits me. They're tying us up. Keeping us busy so they can do... what?

A shadow falls on me as the rumbling sound grows louder. A transport ship hovers overhead. Heavy weapons are mounted underneath it. It's moving slow, because it has to, or for some other reason I don't know, but those guns are trained on our home.

The destruction they could rain down strikes fear into my hearts.

We have to stop it!

"Look!" Ragnar yells, pointing up.

Pain explodes in my left leg. Hissing I look and see a sword protruding. Turning to the opponent, I punch him in the face, and there is a satisfying crunch from beneath his helmet. He stumbles backwards and falls on his back.

The remaining four pause in the press of their attacks, circling, but keeping me from moving towards the wall. Out of the corner of my eye I see Ragnar is surrounded but Arawn is free and running. Resignation settles over me with cold chills. Everything depends on him. If we can't protect our females then we are lost.

The bijass consumes my thoughts and I welcome it, retreating to primal instinct. Fight or flee. I never flee.

They're afraid to approach. I can taste their fear on the air.

It's the sweetest elixir on my tongue. Smiling I make a slow turn on one heel keeping them all within the range of my vision. Spinning my lochaber before me, looking for an opening.

They've all drawn swords, holding them before them in threatening poses. One lowers the tip of his sword, it's a small dip, but all the opening I need.

He's to my left and slightly behind me. I brace my right foot on the ground and push off, spreading my wings, leaping into the air to avoid forcing my injured left to work. Raising the lochaber over my head, I grip it two-handed, and slam it into him. He tries to raise his sword to block, but he's too late.

He falls to the ground, a broken plaything, discarded and useless.

Their circle is broken, and I don't wait for their reaction. Running, each step causing blinding pain as my left leg protests, I break out of their trap.

Dodging from side to side, I turn towards the caves. The air hums, alive with building electricity. The guns on the hovering ship crackle with life.

I'm too late.

They're going to fire. Any second it will be over and there's nothing I can do.

An empty pit in my stomach yawns wide. Bile rises in my throat. I open my mouth to scream but a small belch of fire is all that comes out.

No matter that it's useless, I run.

"MAEVE!" I scream.

Her face floats in front of the fog encompassing my thoughts, drifts across my vision. She is followed by the others. The rest of my Tribe, the humans who live with us. All under our protection. My protection. I'm going to fail.

Impossible.

Blue lightning dances at the end of the massive gun on the ship, coalescing, about to strike.

Maybe, if I leap into the air, if I glide, maybe I can reach them. My leg gives out as I leap. My wings spread, but I'm not high enough to catch the current. The bad jump causes me to tilt to one side. I land hard on the loose sand, tumbling.

Pain. I roll with the impact the best I can, coming to a stop on my feet in time to see the blue lightning of the gunfire.

The world stops.

Silence falls across the desert, no more the clang of steel or the grunts of warriors. Nothing but that deadly crackle as the bolt races down towards our people.

It's over.

I've failed. Black despair crashes over me.

The bolt races down, and then, suddenly, an amber glow appears, and the blast disperses across it, harmless.

Disbelief is quickly followed by resolve.

The shield! Errol must have gotten it working.

Cheers ring out across the battlefield as my brethren shout their elation. My own voice is with theirs, and strangely, the connection I feel to them is deeper. So deep it cuts through the fog of the bijass and primal instinct.

On my feet still, I run for the wall. The Invaders aren't giving up, and press towards the gate. It will not hold against a concerted effort, so that is where help is most needed.

My focus is total. The rest of the world fades to dim awareness as I run, gritting my teeth against the white-hot flashes of pain. Every time I press down with my left leg it screams and tries to give.

I reach down and grab the hilt of the protruding sword. Closing my eyes, I inhale deeply, then jerk it free of my leg. Red-white stars explode across my vision.

None of it stops me. My people are in danger, and pain can be experienced later, when they are safe. None will lay hands on Maeve, or any that are mine.

Lochaber gripped in my left hand, short sword in my right, blood pouring from the open wound in my leg, I open my eyes, spread my wings and hiss a challenge to all that oppose me.

I am here.

"Face me!" I shout and the Invaders at the gate turn towards me.

They struggle to bring their guns to bear. Their hands tremble, and I see the quake in their arms. Their fear is intoxicating, dulling the agony of my leg.

They fire, but it's wide and reckless. They're not aiming but trying to create a field of fire that will hold me back.

Nothing will stop me.

A couple of their shots ting off of my scales, hitting with bruising impact and burning as they ricochet off. They're not prepared to face a Zmaj.

Closing, I fight them two-handed. The short sword and my lochaber create a chaos of blood among their numbers.

Swing, cut, dodge, it's a song of motion, and I lose myself inside of its sweet sound. Pain is distant, belonging to someone else. There is only me against them.

They keep coming. There is no knowing how many of them I've injured or driven away. There is always another before me.

Pressing, pushing, I'm backed up until I'm in the gate itself, holding the line against them.

Beyond them I'm aware, if peripherally, of my brothers fighting. The ones in front of me are all that matter. These are mine to dispatch. These are the ones that would threaten what is mine.

A pounding sound cuts through the haze of battle. Repeating, loud, thundering, it hits against my chest with a force of its own.

In a moment of respite, I look for its source. The ship continues to hover. It's firing, rapidly, pounding against the makeshift shield.

In that instant the shield flickers. It's about to fail, unable to hold up to the barrage.

"Ragnar!" I yell for my brother.

He looks over his shoulder, but he has multiple Invaders he is facing. All of them do.

"The ship!" I yell, pointing with my lochaber.

He nods, and I see the others look as well. I have to do something.

"I've got this!" Maeve yells.

Cold water could not shock me more than hearing her voice. My opponents press in, trying to get past my defense. Strategically I retreat to inside the wall but stopping just inside the gate.

It forces them to come at me no more than three at a time and allows me to see Maeve.

She's running towards Errol, arms loaded with meteorite glass, a flat-out sprint. Sweat pours down her beautiful, perfect face, which is flushed bright red. She's huffing, her lithe legs pounding the ground.

Overhead the shield flickers and fails for a moment, coming back barely in time to stop a bolt from the ship.

Something whistles past my head and there's an explosion next to Maeve. Shards of rock blast out, cutting her face, as a bullet slams into the cliff wall close to her.

"NO!" I scream. Red rage covers my vision.

Dropping the short sword, both hands on my lochaber, I attack with full fury.

The three pushing through the gate stumble back into those behind them, cowed by my renewed assault. Those behind them block their retreat, and I drop all three before they can mount any defense.

None hurt her. None.

Several Invaders stare at me. Too many for a count, the rage won't allow time for that. We stare at each other across the carnage I made of their compatriots.

Raising the lochaber I hold it before me and settle into a defensive stance.

"Bring it," I hiss.

They don't move. Almost as one, they glance at each other, then slowly back away.

Rumbling overhead, the ship retreats too. They don't

bother with the fallen, leaving them lying on the ground as they back away, never taking their eyes off me.

Moving forward, I press the advantage, but they don't respond, except to move faster in their haste to escape. The rest of their attack force does the same, moving away from the other Zmaj.

Distantly their ship settles onto a dune and a gangplank lowers, picking them up.

As it lifts into the air and darts away, a cheer rises, and I join the celebration, adding my voice to our victory, but I don't wait to run back beyond the wall, directly to Errol's machine, where I saw Maeve.

Maeve stands bent over with her hands on her knees, panting heavily.

"Are you okay?" I ask the moment I'm close enough for her to hear me.

"Yeah," she huffs, not looking up.

Her face is very red yet pale. Moisture drips off of it, pattering against the hard-packed sand.

"She saved us," Errol says, admiration in his voice. "It was her quick thinking to add more glass to the machine."

"It... was... nothing," she says, gasping air between words.

"No, it was everything," he says. "Very brave."

Errol's eyes lock onto mine as he says the last words. He nods his understanding. He means what he says is the highest compliment he can give. Maeve glances to him with a wan smile, finally straightening, inhaling deeply, and nodding.

"Damn, I need to work out more," she exhales heavily.

Errol laughs, shaking his head. Her fear dissipates as she stands. In some unknowable manner I sense it parting like clouds moving away from the sun. She smiles, a full, real smile, and it is brighter than both the suns combined.

"How bad—" she cuts off midsentence, her eyes landing on my leg, widening. "You're hurt!"

"It's nothing," I say, glancing at my leg.

Blood soaks my pants through and now I'm certain of her safety, the pain throbs sharply. The muscles strain, threatening to give out, causing me to wobble.

"It's not nothing," she admonishes, kneeling before me before I can respond.

Her delicate hands tear at the fabric of my pants exposing the wound. A large gash down my thigh, scales poke out where the sword tore through them to find purchase in my flesh.

"A bandage is all I need," I protest.

She looks up at me, her face unreadable but cloudy with a storm of emotions. She shakes her head, lips pursed, brow furrowed, and eyes narrowed.

"Do not be a fool," she says. "Come with me, now."

There is no resisting her control, and in truth, I don't want to. It's not the pain, though it is there, it's all her intention. Her control is absolute, unwavering. Control any male would be proud to exert over those around him. She is dominant.

I submit to her.

It's strange. A sensation of being out of place, as if the world is the same yet completely new at the same time blankets across me as I follow her to my own cave, doing my best to not limp. I've never, in my life, submitted to another. It's foreign to me.

She pushes me around, settling me onto my bench then taking up cleaning supplies and healing paste. Silently, she works the wound over. I watch her as she dabs at the wound carefully. She glances up occasionally to see how I'm doing, I assume.

As she works, her concern is a thick emotion that beats

inside of me the same as I feel her heartbeat in my head, beating in time with my own.

"There, that's clean," she says, her voice low, sweet and raspy.

Desire blossoms at the sound of it. It suddenly strikes me we're alone in my sleeping cave, and the thought immediately turns into raging desire. I need her, physically, emotionally, in ways I could never admit to myself or anyone else. She is... everything.

A raging inferno deep inside myself, deeper than, more than my body she is my treasure. The bijass rushes forward, pushing the need to make her mine, but that instinct I will never give in to. I am myself, I am more than those base instincts.

Resisting them or not, they do enhance and entice the very real desire I feel for her. Desire that I know she cannot be unaware of, for it tents out my pants, mere inches from her face. Studiously, she doesn't acknowledge my obvious arousal.

She swallows hard, her eyes darting towards the tent, and a sudden tight sensation grips my chest, but it doesn't seem to be mine. She finishes tying a bandage around the wound then rises to her feet. Pointedly her eyes are locked on mine, not even glancing down.

"There," she says, her voice sounds rough, almost gravelly.

"Thank you," I say, not rising because this way we are almost eye to eye.

The feeling it creates in me when I look straight into her eyes like this is something I want to hold on to. Everything about her is shifting my own thoughts. She is strange and alien and everything I never knew I wanted or needed.

If only she would submit to me as I am submitting to her. If only...

"I should... go," she says.

An instant, quick as the darting attack of a zmeya, her eyes drop to my arousal before she plants them firmly back on my eyes. Her lips part, full, lush, and I want to kiss them with every fiber of my being. Taste her, lay claim to them and through them to her.

Words fail.

Words are weak. This situation requires steel. Steel, hard, unyielding, giving in to no demands until I force my will on it.

Steel, I understand. Words... I've never been good with them.

Eyes locked on hers too, I reach and place my hands on her shoulders. She trembles under my touch but doesn't pull away. My cock pulses, shaking with need, the fire inside is a raging inferno, and she is the only thing that will keep it from consuming me.

Slowly my eyes drop to her soft lips. Gently I pull her forward. She bends, yielding to my pressure, coming closer until her sweet breath passes over my skin.

She pulls back, shaking her head an instant before our lips touch.

"I've got to go," she says, spinning on her heel and rushing out of the room.

My room is emptier now than it was before she was inside it. It's an emptiness that aches inside me, accented by the raging need of my cock. The hanging cloth over the door is still swaying from her swift exit. The scent of her sweet breath still fills my nostrils. She dominates my thoughts.

Left hanging, my cock fully engorged, with a burning need in my core, I rise to my feet and try to shift my thoughts away from her.

It's impossible. My dick throbs, demanding relief. I reach under the tie of my pants and take my engorged member in my hand. It pulses in my hand as if anticipating the release to come. I close my eyes. The image of her awaits in the dark privacy of my mind. The sweet scent of her skin, her full, lush lips—I can imagine how soft they would be on mine.

My cock stiffens harder still. I grip it in one hand and pull, moving my hand towards the tip, applying pressure to the soft underside. The skin shifts under my grip, and pleasure rips its way from my stiff member up and into my thoughts.

Slowly moving my hand up and down the shaft, I imagine what she will taste like. What she would look like without the protective layer of clothing. The softness of her skin under my fingers. Tracing the lines of her lips with my tongue.

My hand moves faster as I imagine kissing my way down her neck towards the mounds that her blouses always hide. I want to know what those mounds look like. Strange and alien? The mated males say little to nothing about it, but if the topic does come up, they have a knowing smile that says more than words ever will.

She kneels before me, lowering herself before my raging erection. Her small hands, too small to encompass all of my girth, grip my cock and stroke. It's not my hand on me, it's hers. My balls tighten as the sensation of pending explosion increases.

In my mind's eye, she is touching, exploring, rubbing my member, but I want to pleasure her. Need to hear her crying out her excitement.

Taking her arms, I gently lift her and lay her on our bed. One I will make special for her, overstuffed, comfortable, hugging her delicate body. Her pants slide over her hips, exposing the fur between her legs. This much the mated males have shared, and the idea of it is almost as exotic as the mounds on her chest.

It will smell of her, I'm sure. I lower myself between her

legs and both give and take of her moisture. Tasting her, finding the parts of her that most pleasure her. Bringing her to the edge of the ultimate pleasure.

My dick jumps in my hand then. I can't hold back any longer. It spasms in welcome release, one that brings more pleasure than any time previous. A shudder runs up and down my spine before the orgasm releases me, but I'm left empty. Now I wish stronger than ever that I had Maeve here beside me to hold. To stroke her smooth skin, to rest my hand on her silky hair, to breathe the scents of her body. To keep her safe beside me all through the night. Her absence leaves me emptier now than I was before I ever saw her.

Maeve. How do I show you what we can be?

Dinner time comes, and I join the rest of the Tribe at our communal dining. The gate sustained damage during the attack, and its repairs kept me busy for the afternoon. Coming through the line and filling my plate, I'm painfully aware of Maeve.

Everything about her calls to me, but I'm reluctant to look at her. Uncertainty about us creates a feeling of walking on shifting sand. I have no doubt she's feeling the same desires I am, but she's not acting on them. It's clear the moment our eyes dart across each other. The echoing beat of her heart in the back of my head speeds up, racing, and my own hearts answer.

She is talking with Delilah, too soft for me to hear far ahead of me in the line. Once I've filled my plate the only open seat is several people away from those two. Perhaps it is best, maybe she needs space and time. What else can I do but abide by what I think her wishes are?

The bijass pulses with primal urges, capture her, take her

away and keep her until she knows she is mine and we belong together.

Primal, primitive, not who I am, no matter how appealing any avenue that results in us together might be. Even if I did such a thing, it would only backfire. No male will force himself on a female, and I don't believe Maeve would be swayed by any such efforts. No, she is a creature of a completely different metal.

No, she's not metal. She's fire.

Nodding to myself, I focus on my food, half-listening to Drosdan talk about the attack. A lot of back-and-forth happens, but my thoughts constantly drift away from it. Any lull is an excuse, and they're drawn to Maeve and how to resolve the demands of my dragon nature with what she wants.

Before the meteorite shower this was much easier because I didn't think she actually wanted me. I was resigned to being alone, not indulging my dragon. Now, there is no doubt in my mind she wants me. My awareness of her, what she feels, is as clear as my awareness of my own tail.

That her actions are completely different than what I know she is feeling makes no sense. That is what I struggle to comprehend. How can she act different than what desire would demand of us?

"We have to report to Visidion and Rosalind," Maeve says, her sultry, raspy voice jerking my attention out of the circuitous thoughts.

"Of course," Drosdan agrees. "But not yet. First, we need to make sure we're safe. An initial test of the device isn't enough to say it works. It barely held against the assault."

"If it hadn't…" Olivia doesn't finish the sentence.

"The wall was damaged," Errol observes. "We'll need to effect repairs."

"None of which prevents one or two of us from going to the City to report," Maeve counters.

Her eyes flash brilliantly, her mouth is set, and her brazenness shines as she holds her ground against any and all comers. How can I do anything but admire her?

"One or two isn't safe," Olivia adds.

"We shouldn't travel in less than pairs, trios would be better, especially if we're taking humans," Melchior says. "That way they can't go after a weak link."

"We're not weak links," Maeve exclaims, bristling.

"I was about to say the same," Lana adds, glaring at Melchior.

There's no stopping the smile that spreads across my face. Maeve's fiery attitude is red-hot and beautiful. She's like my forge, red-hot and ready to bend any steel.

"Trios is a good idea," Drosdan says, ending that topic with finality.

The conversation carries on well into the night until at last, three are chosen to go to the City while we effect repairs and see what can be done to strengthen the shield that covers our home. After scraping my plate off and putting it in for washing, I turn and all but run over Maeve.

"Sorry," I say, side-stepping to avoid hitting her.

"It's fine," she says, her eyes darting to mine, then away.

She steps around me and adds her plate to the stack. Her hand lingers on it before she turns and looks at me. Feeling oddly uncomfortable, I shift from foot to foot, unsure what to say, but not wanting to leave her presence.

"How's the leg?" she asks, cutting through the swirling thoughts.

"Hmm? Oh, right!" I look down at it and shift my weight back onto it, testing its feel. "Better. Thank you."

"Good," she says, nodding and biting her lower lip. She still isn't looking directly at me.

"Are you... okay?" I struggle to find words, anything to keep the conversation going now that it's started.

I want to hear her voice, listen to her words, gain any insight I can into her thoughts.

"Yeah," she says, crossing her arms over her chest. "Frustrated, but I'm fine."

"Frustrated?" I ask, probing.

"Yeah," she says, shaking her head. "You, men."

She snaps the last word then, for the first time, she meets my eyes, and she laughs. It's infectious, and a moment after she starts, I'm laughing too. I don't know why, have no understanding of what we're laughing at or about, but it feels good. We're doing it together, and I won't trade that for the world.

We walk, together, a silent invitation implied, if nothing else, by the fact she doesn't head in a different direction. Our laughter trails off and a comfortable silence falls. The suns are set, the stars are out above in a clear sky. As we walk past the garden, the scents of fresh vegetables and turned earth drift past my nostrils, and somehow it serves to accent the subtle scent of her.

"Maeve," I say, praying my next words don't break this spell.

"Yes?" she asks.

"Tell me about your ship. Tell me about your home."

She doesn't say anything. We walk several steps while I wait, pinpricks of anticipation racing across my scales. Have I said the wrong thing? Asked too much?

"What would you like to know?" she asks, finally.

"Everything," I say, my throat clenching tight with emotion.

"That's a lot," she laughs.

"It is," I say, considering. "Why would... how did you leave your home?"

I know from the other human females the story of their generation ship, but I want to hear Maeve's thoughts.

"I didn't," she says. "I was born on the ship. It's the only world I ever knew. My great-great grandparents made the choice," she says. "Their choices set all our fates in motion."

"Strange, why would they make such a decision?" I ask, trying to imagine leaving Tajss with no intention of ever seeing it again.

Maeve smiles, looking up at me, and her bright eyes reflect the starlight, dancing with joy.

"Earth, our home, was overpopulated. Extremely so, they had more mouths to feed than they could possibly manage. The moon and even another nearby planet had been terraformed—you know, made like Earth—and turned almost exclusively into farms, but it still wasn't enough. The population boom had taken its toll.

The planet was failing. So they built the generation ships. We had no inhabitable planets close to us, but if we could plan generations into the future? Then we could send ahead terraforming robots and when the population arrived, we'd come home to a fully prepared planet. A bit of our own heaven."

She is opening up to me! I must keep her talking. "It sounds frightening," I say. "Leaving your home on the hopes of a dream that you will never see yourself."

"Yeah," she says, hugging herself tightly. "I used to lie awake late at night sometimes thinking about making that decision. How bad was it, really? I think it was even worse than what we were taught."

"You were taught?" I gently prod, drinking in her inner thoughts with relish.

"Oh sure," she says. "We had school growing up, regular classes including Earth History. Plus, we had the vids for entertainment."

"What are... vids?" I roll the word off my tongue trying to make sure I pronounce it correctly.

"Vids are-- were moving pictures that tell stories, I guess is the best way to put them. My ancestors were smart enough to foresee the biggest problem we were going to have on the ship was boredom. You can't expect people to work all day, every day for their entire lives. What do we do when we're not working?

"So they packed it full of entertainment. We had no way to make new entertainment, so they made sure we had fully loaded libraries of every kind and color. Music, movies, what they called television shows, anything and everything so we would have something to do.

"Of course, it's also all new with each generation so it's kind of an unlimited resource."

"Oh," I say, not positive I understand.

I don't recall anything like this on Tajss, even before the Devastation. Perhaps I don't remember, and it did exist. So much of my memory is lost to the fog of the bijass.

"Was there not something like it on Tajss, you know, before?" she asks, curiosity coloring her voice, beautiful eyes fixed on me with genuine interest.

Suddenly I'm uncomfortable. Admitting how little of "before" I remember is painful. It's a weakness to not know one's past.

We've stopped outside the cave she calls home, about halfway up the cliff face following the path that we've smoothed out. At this vantage we can look out over the wall, across the empty desert of Tajss. The wide-open sky, bright with twinkling stars, lays over the rolling dunes of sand like a blanket. An expansion in my chest causes my hearts to skip a beat as I look out across my home.

"Perhaps," I say, not answering the question directly.

Maeve places a hand on my arm, soft and warm, but

doesn't press the question. I wonder if she understands my reluctance? A soft sensation flows across my scales, starting from where she touches.

Gazing at her hand, small and delicate, is fascinating, absorbing all my attention. Her heart pounds in the back of my head, and my own hearts match its pace. Pulling my eyes up, I meet hers and see the open desire in them.

"Good night," she says, but I know without any doubt she wants to say something different.

The dragon in my soul roars, wanting her to speak aloud, needing her to invite me in. Her lips part, she's going to say the words. There is something magnetic between us, a pulling, driving us together.

Say it!

Her lips close, she smiles, then removes her hand. She steps through the makeshift door of leather, and it drops heavily into place.

An empty ache in my core holds me there, staring at the cured leather, holding out hope she'll open it once more and invite me in.

I don't know how long I stand there before it becomes clear that's not going to happen. I turn and head for my own bed.

Alone.

7

MAEVE

*I*t's ridiculous. No way, not him. Any of them but him.

I toss over onto my side, pull the blanket up around my neck, and snuggle in deeper.

I can't get the look in Padraig's eyes out of my thoughts. The way his scales felt under my touch. Cool, hard, yet somehow erotic in a way I could never have imagined.

When I touch him, there's an electric pulse between us. I'm not stupid, I know he wants me. Which is fine, all in all, but what am I doing wanting him?

Him!

Ugh. He's so... masculine?

No, wrong. He's too male, he's overbearing, hard-headed, stubborn, and he thinks women are weak. How could I be with a man who won't treat me as an equal? Listen to my thoughts?

Except he did, didn't he?

Is there more to him than I've seen?

Obviously, don't be daft, Maeve.

Why can't I sleep?

Tossing over the other way again, I hear Delilah stir on her bed, and then suddenly she sits up.

"All right, out with it," she demands, her voice heavy with broken sleep.

"Sorry, it's nothing," I say.

"If it was nothing, you wouldn't be tossing and turning so much you're keeping me awake. So talk it out, let's get this done so I can sleep!"

Sitting up on my bed I pull my knees up to my chest and wrap my arms around them. No matter the gruffness of her words, I know she cares and wants to help.

What do I say? Do I tell her everything? Nothing? Some or all?

"It's Padraig," I say, trying to figure out what to say and what not to say.

"That much is obvious," she says, shaking her head. "What about him? He's big, sexy, and obviously head over heels for you, what's the problem?"

I stare at her in the dim light. I can't see her face well enough to read her expression, but I know mine is one of shock. How can she make it so simple? She knows how he is!

"The problem is..." I trail off unsure what it is. "He's.... him."

Lame. Good job Maeve, way to put it out there with a clearly articulated argument.

"He's dominating, controlling, and he's flat-out mean a lot of times."

"Is he to you?" she asks.

"Sometimes?" even I hear the questioning note in my response.

He's never been mean to me, not actually, chauvinistic, yes but never mean.

"Really?" she asks.

"No, sort of, gah!"

"Right," Delilah says. "He likes you. He's a man. More than that, he's a Zmaj. They've all got their issues, like any man does. You've got to be woman enough to hold your own against him and help him become what he can be, more than what he is."

Her words shock me into silence, cutting through all the noise in my head.

"I've never looked at it like that," I say, at last.

"Of course not," she says. "It's my idea."

She comes over to my bed and sits next to me. After putting her arm around my shoulders, she pulls me against her. I rest my head on her shoulder and sigh.

"Thanks," I say, gratitude a swelling tide overwhelming me.

"Sure," she says. "What can I say? I'm jealous. I want a sexy Zmaj to make me his own."

She laughs but behind that laugh I sense a hint of empty loneliness.

"It will happen," I assure her.

"I don't know," she says, in a moment of frank honesty. "We're running out of men."

That sits heavy in the room, silencing any further conversation. She turns her head, kisses my forehead, then moves back to her own bed.

"Sleep," she orders.

Lying down my thoughts aren't the same as they were. Now I'm thinking about my friend and her loneliness. I want to help her, somehow.

At some point, I finally fall asleep.

It's been days since Padraig and I had our walk under the stars. We see each other and it's comfortable but brief. He's busy repairing the gate and damage done during the attack. I'm busy making candles, prepping vegetables, and in general life has gone on.

I'm not sure what our next move is, but I do see he's changing. He's even different with the other Zmaj than he was. Less gruff and overall not being a jerk to everyone.

On one hand it's strange. Padraig was a source of constancy in my universe. He was what he was, you knew what you were getting when you dealt with him. This new Padraig is an unknown.

He's different, yes, but what does that mean for me? Is he different enough?

He's still gruff, and there is no doubt in my mind he still holds his views on women in general. Ugh, I don't know what to think about it.

Tearing the leaves off the vegetable in my hand I toss it into the box with the others and reach for the next one. Delilah works across from me, strangely silent today. I've been so lost in my thoughts I've hardly noticed it, but it suddenly hits me that she's barely said a word all morning.

"Are you okay?" I ask.

She looks up from her work, sighs, then shakes her head.

"I could ask the same," she counters.

"Sure," I agree. "But we always talk about me, let's talk about you."

I laugh to take the edge off of the truth. My relationship with Padraig and my complete lack of a love life has been the most common topic of conversation between us for days now. She smiles and shrugs.

"I don't know," she says.

"Yeah?" I push.

"Yeah," she says, staring at the vegetable in her hand. "It's... monotonous. This is our life, now."

"Sure, but it's not so bad is it?" I ask.

"Isn't it? I don't know. Sometimes it's all so... melancholy, I guess. It's one day after another and no matter how much we try to paint a pretty picture of it, we're one step away from not making it."

"You're right," I say. "It's not easy."

"That's it, right? Every day we're struggling to survive. We cover it over with routines and jobs and keeping busy but this planet..."

Her voice trails off with unspoken words that sit heavy between us. I know what she means, of course. Life here isn't just hard, it's damn near impossible. The fact we've survived at all is a miracle, but staying that way, well that takes miracles to an entirely new level.

"Well," I say. "We are making it."

"Yeah, we are," she smiles.

It's a wan smile—I know it, she knows it—but it's a smile. There's nothing I can say that's going to change things. Instead I walk around to her side of the worktable and pull her into a tight hug.

"We got this," I say, holding her tight. She returns the embrace, then we go back to our work. "Trust me, it could be worse. I'm not sure how, mind you, but I have absolute faith it can be."

"True," she says. "We could be living under that asshole Gershom."

"Or Annabel," I counter, both of us laughing.

It lightens the mood a lot. Which we need. It also pulls my thoughts away from the hamster's wheel that is Padraig.

A shout from outside cuts through our levity. Wordlessly, we're both running out of the cave to see what is happening. Overhead, the now familiar shielding blinks, then there's a loud pop, and it's gone.

Smoke drifts across the commons from Errol's workshop.

"No!" Errol's cry of despair echoes off the cliff walls.

Everyone is out and looking. No one moves, all of us staring at the rolling black smoke column that drifts out and up.

"Oh, no," Delilah says.

"This is bad," I observe.

Padraig runs from the gate where he's been working towards Errol's workshop. Watching him move awakens latent desire. His massive muscles bunch and release as he moves. His tail swings, his wings open up, and he leaps, gliding with a surprising grace for his size.

He lands running and is the first to disappear into the smoke. The other Zmaj run as well, but all of them are slower than he was.

Is that the way he's always been? Is it another change?

He emerges from the smoke with Errol in his arms. Cold fear races through my limbs then I'm running too.

"Is he?" I cry out.

"He's fine," Padraig says. "I think."

Gently he lays Errol down on the ground. Errol coughs and rolls to one side, leaning up on his elbow. He coughs more, a rough sound, and wipes at his eyes. His scales are stained with dark soot.

"I'm fine," he says, pushing himself to a full sitting position.

"How bad is the machine?" Drosdan asks, pushing his way through the crowd. Drosdan dwarfs even Padraig, dominating the space with his huge size.

"I don't know," Padraig says, coughing more. "I'd say not good."

"What happened?" Drosdan asks the question we're all wondering.

The crowd pushes in to hear the answer. Poor Errol probably needs air, but our survival hinges on that shield working. How else can we stand against the invaders when they bring ships against us?

"That machine isn't designed for this," he says. "I'm doing the best I can but it's not my training. It's meant for short, ship-to-ship battles. Getting it to work non-stop, you see the result."

Drosdan nods, tree-trunk arms crossed over his huge barrel chest.

"What do you need?" he asks.

"I have to talk with Addison," he says. "She understands this machine better than I do."

"Fine, let's make it happen," Drosdan says. He looks at the circling crowd.

"Until we have the machine back and working, we're on lockdown. No one goes outside the wall. Move all work possible into the main cave. Let's also move the workstations in deeper.

"The less attention we draw if they do a flyover the better."

A murmur of assent runs through the crowd, then without further discussion everyone departs and starts to work.

Padraig and I lock eyes for a moment, and the now familiar magnetic pulse hits me. I notice his eyes widen—he feels it too.

Instinctively my hand drops to my side, resting on the meteorite glass embedded into me. It throbs almost as if it's alive.

Tearing my eyes away from Padraig, I turn and follow Delilah to do the work Drosdan ordered. My heart pounds and my breath comes shallow. The double echo in the back of my skull mirrors the fast pace of my heart.

It's amazing, strange, and so different. Maybe I should talk to Addison about what's happening. Or Delilah, or someone. Am I feeling real things, or is it some strange influence of the glass embedded into me?

I don't know, but the work before us is what matters, and having something to focus on is more helpful than worrying about it.

We move craft tables, work stations, and everything possible as deep into the massive cavern as possible. It's much darker, so we're going to go through candles a lot faster than we have been, meaning even more work.

There isn't any alternative, and we're all resigned to it. As we wrap up the work, the stations are close to the crack in the rear of the cavern that leads down into the tunnel where the men harvest epis. The soft blue-purple glow of the life-giving plant is visible through the opening, but it's nowhere near enough light to work by, unfortunately.

"Whew," I say, wiping sweat off my forehead. "That was hard."

"Yeah," Delilah says, putting her hands on her lower back and stretching.

"I'm ready for dinner," I observe.

"You and me both," she says.

Drosdan had the communal tables moved inside the cave as well, but they're set up closer to the entrance, so we have the fresher air and the soft light of the night sky to eat by. I'm glad. Eating deep in the cave is too much. It's cloistered and oppressive to not have fresh air around me, especially when I'm eating.

Dinner is fast and somber tonight. Normally it's alive, bright with conversation about the day and whatever, but not now. Everyone is worried about the loss of the machine. The recent attack by the Invaders has made it clear we're in more danger than we even knew.

"What do they want?" Olivia asks, breaking the heavy silence.

No one asks what she means. We've all got the same question.

"Epis," Drosdan says. "It has to be."

"Then why the attacks on the mining settlement? Why not the City?"

"Too protected?" Ragnar offers.

"We have too many questions," Drosdan says. "For now we must focus on safety. Then we'll buy ourselves time to answer them."

"Right," Melchior agrees. "We should patrol tonight. We don't want to be taken by surprise."

"Good," Drosdan nods. "Volunteers?"

"I will," Padraig says.

All the Zmaj offer to take turns, and they quickly work out a series of shifts. Dinner breaks up, and we all finish the last of our daily chores, cleaning dishes, storing supplies and such. As I walk out of the cave, heading for my bed, Padraig steps up beside me.

"Maeve," he says, and instantly a shiver runs down my spine, my mouth is dry, my throat is tight, and desire burns hot in my core.

"Padraig," I barely manage to say his name. My thoughts are clouded by need. It colors everything. His deep, rolling bass voice caresses my skin, igniting fire as it touches me deeper than a voice has any right to.

He doesn't say anything more. We stand, inches apart, our bodies pulling towards each other against any hint of sense.

My lips tremble as my hand betrays my better judgment, reaching for him.

When I touch the scales of his arm, they're cool. Hard, yet strangely erotic. The desire flames higher. Suddenly it's an inferno that can't be contained.

Padraig grabs me, sweeping me up in his massive arms,

lifting me into him. His lips smash against mine, bruising, commanding yet somehow in all the roughness he's gentle.

His tongue forces its way into my mouth before I can open. Invading, taking what we both want.

Gripping my ass, he squeezes, and his erection digs into my lower stomach, pulsing with need. I wrap my arms around his neck, and he carries me away.

I'm lost in the kiss. Unaware of our surroundings, throwing caution to the wind.

My body responds to him, becoming a quivering betrayer to all that I know should matter, it doesn't care. It wants this. No, I need this.

It's been so long since I've taken a lover, since before the crash. It's high time to end my enforced celibacy. We can sort out the ramifications later.

My tongue wrestles with his, then we're up against a wall. His massive body pinning me there. Wrapping my legs around his waist I grind against his bulging cock, wanting it inside me so badly I'm moaning.

He hisses softly. His hands fumble at my blouse, but unable to get it undone, he rips the soft fabric, tearing it off of me and tossing it to one side.

My nipples, already erect, ache as they brush against his rough scales.

His hands cover them, protective, then he's kneading my breasts while his hips make a small thrusting motion against my burning pussy.

"Yes!" I cry out as he flicks one nipple, and his hardness finds its way to apply pressure to my clit.

Stars explode in my head, blasting away everything.

Driving my hands between us, I find the waist of his pants and undo the tie, letting them drop to the floor. His lips never part from mine. His tongue never retreats from my mouth. He's staked his claim and I've welcomed him in.

Hips grinding and thrusting, my hand finds his cock. It's hard, harder than anything I've experienced before. It takes me a moment to realize that the top side of his dick has ridges running along its length.

It gives me a moment's pause. Underneath, the bottom side is soft, stiff, but more like a man's cock.

It doesn't matter. I must have satisfaction. I know that this will work—it's not like I'm the first girl to fuck a Zmaj.

Pushing aside the fear and doubt, I stroke the length of his shaft.

Padraig groans into our kiss. The thrust of his hips becomes more insistent. His hands grip my tits harder, squeezing tightly.

Roughly, he pulls me off the wall, carrying me to the bed. After tossing me onto it, he stands over me, massive, dominating, and controlling. Welcoming him, I lift my hips as he pulls my pants off.

His cock stands erect before him, bulging, jumping of its own accord in time with the beating of his hearts that thrum in the back of my head.

The pieces of meteorite glass embedded in his scales pulse and shine as if with a light of their own. Wetness floods my inner folds, preparing the way for him.

He looks down at me and in his eyes, I see so much more than desire. Reflected in them I see, for a moment, what he sees, and it makes me feel beautiful.

Slowly, almost teasingly, he lowers himself between my legs. His fingers trail softly up my thighs. Goosebumps follow the trail of them as he moves closer to my core.

He leans in, warm breath passing over my mound, and I shiver in response. Grabbing his head, I wrap my fingers in his hair and jerk him forward.

I can't wait any longer.

His hot mouth crashes against my wetness, and his tongue divides my folds.

"Yes!" I scream, unable to contain the sensations of pleasure that rip through me.

His tongue does things I can't comprehend. Driving in, up, down, around—it's everywhere, parting every fold, exploring every part of me.

The tightness in my lower stomach becomes too much and in what seems only moments I'm pushed over the edge.

The orgasm rips my world apart with an intensity that I can't believe.

"I'm coming!" I shout, to him, to the world.

Sex has never been this good. He doesn't let up. If anything, he drives harder. His tongue pushing the sensations higher, stronger, and I'm sure I'll explode.

Tightening my grip, my back arching, my toes curl so tight it hurts until at last it passes, and I collapse. Heaving, muscles left weak and trembling, barely able to convince my fingers to ease my grip on his hair.

Looking up at me from between my legs, his eyes alight with delight, he smiles.

Slowly, showing an incredible restraint, he rises onto his arms and climbs up across me. Watching him move, his cock dangling between us like a divining rod seeking its own pleasure.

It approaches, coming closer.

My body is ready. Already.

The most powerful orgasm I've ever experienced, and my body wants more.

I want more.

I want him.

Need him.

He moves closer, and I spread my legs, welcoming him. His lips trail hot kisses up across my body, moving closer.

The tip of his massive, throbbing cock presses against the quivering flesh of my mound.

Pressing forward, he penetrates slowly, his lips claiming mine again. I taste myself on him. It's oddly erotic, a scent and taste that enhances the pleasure as his ribbed dick pushes into my slick tunnel, forcing me open, widening me.

Using deliberate pressure he drives into me, and my body takes his girth without problem. Welcoming him as if he's coming home after too long gone.

It pulls my focus fully to the two of us joining. The beating of his hearts in my head races along as my own gallops to join the rhythm.

He seats himself fully into me and warmth flashes along my side, where the glass resides. The room lightens as the glass flashes.

My fingers trail across the glass embedded in him and something snaps. It's not a sound but a feeling, a sensation. An awareness of him and myself, of a connection between us.

His fire burns into me, it's an inferno inside him, his dragon. Desire, need, something more than there are words to describe.

He needs me.

Treasure.

In his thoughts, I am his treasure.

It flashes through as the pleasure of his cock filling me pushes other thoughts aside.

He pulls back, exerting remarkable control, then he thrusts into me twice, three times before we give ourselves over to wild abandon.

He grunts as he thrusts. The sounds of his pleasure excite me, filling my ears as his cock fills my pussy.

My hands run over his body, touching him everywhere. He keeps going, his stamina is impressive.

Reaching between us I grab his balls and fondle them as

he continues to push in and out. His eyes snap open in surprise, but then he smiles, thrusting harder.

He drives into me forcefully, pushing me up on the bed until my head is against the wall and he's pounding me over and over. I don't want it to end, even as a fresh orgasm builds.

In one final thrust, he groans loudly.

"Maeve!" he cries out, and then he's filling me.

His cock explodes, spasming inside my pussy over and over until I'm overfull, unable to contain it all.

He holds himself over me, his back arching, and my own orgasm rips through my body.

At last he lowers himself onto me, his bulk and cool scales lying against my skin, absorbing my own fevered nature.

"Amazing," I breathe.

He lies there a moment, breathing heavily, his cock softening inside of me.

After a few moments, he pulls out and moves to lie beside me. Throwing my arms up over my head I bask in the afterglow of great sex. His fingers trail over my chest, down across my stomach and down to my thighs.

He kisses along my cheek, down my neck, and across my shoulder. Shivering I pull away when he hits a ticklish spot.

My eyes journey down his magnificent body. I watch as his cock retreats, then in a moment of stunning surprise, another cock rises in its place.

"What?" I ask, eyes widening in surprise.

He looks where my eyes are looking, obvious confusion on his face.

"What?" he asks, his eyes searching for a threat.

"Your..." I don't know what to say.

He follows my gaze again, and at last his eyes land on his cock.

"Yes?" he asks, as if two cocks is the most normal thing anyone ever heard of.

My body though, it definitely has a different response than my mind is having, as I try to comprehend the entire idea. Wetness is already flowing, and my pussy quivers with anticipation, causing me to shiver for an entirely different reason.

"Two?" I ask, desire clouding rationality.

"Of course," he says, kissing my lips, trailing warmth across my chin, down my neck.

"Of course," I exhale as his ministrations warm me for another round.

How did I not know this was a thing?

8

PADRAIG

*W*hen I wake, she is gone. The bed is still warm where she was and her scent lingers. I roll onto my side, pull the blanket to my face, and inhale her.

Her taste is on my tongue, her scent in my nose, and my dragon growls in pleasure.

She is mine. At last, she is mine.

Then where is she?

Rising onto an elbow and looking around the small room I call home, I see sunlight creeping through the door cover. It's later than I normally sleep if the suns are rising. I dress and splash some water on my face before heading outside.

The Tribe is awake and in motion, as everything should be. I don't see Maeve in the garden area or the grounds. I take a moment to draw my senses inward, and I feel her heart beating in the back of my head. Then I know, somehow, that she's in the main cave.

It's good. Drosdan said we're on lockdown, and that is the safest place for her to be right now.

It's past time for breakfast so I decide to forego it. My work on the gate needs to be finished today, if possible. I'm trying to strengthen the steel so it will stand better against the Invaders' weapons.

No easy task to be sure.

The work is good, consuming, and the glowing pleasure of the previous night warms my insides, just as the fire of the forge warms my scales.

The world seems brighter today. Different. It's a strange feeling. Somehow it feels like there's something ahead. Dimly, in the fog of the bijass, a sensation of loss and being trapped tries to push its way out, but I ignore that.

Nothing is going to change how bright this day is. Maeve is mine. My treasure welcomed me home.

We are together, and nothing else matters. I will protect her no matter the cost.

"Padraig!" Samil yells.

Stopping my hammer on the anvil, the loud clang echoing away, I look at the smaller Zmaj.

Hints of anger dance through my thoughts, but today not even Samil can arouse my ire.

"What?" I ask, not missing the way he flinches when my eyes land on him.

"They want you," he says, looking over his shoulder.

Drosdan is by the wall, and three more of my brethren stand with him. Nodding, I put the hammer down, turn and bank the fire of the forge, then walk over to the others.

Samil trails along behind me, carefully staying out of easy reach. He's learning. One day he might be male enough to take a woman of his own. I hope so, for his sake. No male should be without his treasure.

"Are you sure?" Drosdan is saying.

"Yes," Melchior says. "They're positive. I didn't see it myself, but the miners say there is no doubt of it."

"Why?" Drosdan asks, shaking his head. "Why would they want that? It's not epis?"

"Apparently not," Melchior responds, shaking his head and holding his hands up, palms to the sky, as he shrugs.

"Who wants what?" I ask.

"The Invaders," Melchior says, shaking his head. "They want the glass."

"It's not epis," Arawn muses.

Drosdan grunts and shakes his head. My thoughts spin as I try to figure out what this could mean.

"So..." I say, but the thought won't form into a whole.

The four of us look at each other, and mirrored in their faces is the same confusion I feel.

"It's not epis," Drosdan says, repeating the same thought.

It's the one all of us are thinking. Our memories may be clouded from before the Devastation, but all of us know, with certainty, that epis is the most valuable thing on the planet.

Or it was.

What is it about this glass?

The glass embedded in my scales warms, and the beating of Maeve's heart in the back of my head grows louder, pulling at my attention.

"We can't let them have it," Drosdan says. "If they want it, we need to know more about it."

"Right," I agree, on principle as much as anything.

We stare at each other, silent, deep in our own thoughts. The world is changing almost as much as it did when the humans crashed down.

Nothing makes sense. It leaves the future uncertain and strange. It's not a sensation I'm enjoying. Especially now that Maeve has accepted me as her mate.

I think. We haven't talked about it, but we are lovers. That means something, even to the strange customs of the humans. It's more than nothing, and I am confident it will continue to grow, becoming what it truly should be. She is my fated mate. She is meant to be mine as much as I am meant to be hers. My primal dragon chose her—there is no way around it.

"All right, now what?" Melchior asks. "What do we do about it?"

Silence sits heavily on our group, and moments pass with no one saying a word.

"We have to gather it faster, here and at the mining Village," Drosdan says at last. "Melchior, you take charge of the miners, make them understand that we have to get this done. We'll gather it and bring it here for safekeeping."

"Would it not be safer in the City?" Arawn ventures.

Drosdan glares at him with a deep frown. The tension rises while we wait to see what our de facto leader will say. Arawn is probably right—they have a full, working dome that can resist the Invaders' ships easier than our makeshift one. It doesn't make the insult to a Zmaj pride easier to swallow, and Drosdan is proud if nothing else.

"I'll talk to Visidion," he says at last, dropping his arms to his side.

The tension dissipates with the dropping of his arms. We nod agreement.

"Tell the other males," Drosdan orders. "Keep the humans out of sight. They won't be joining us on gatherings. Too slow, too much of a burden. We can do this faster."

"You want me to go back to the miners now?" Melchior asks.

"Yes," Drosdan nods. "Where's Samil?"

"Up here," Samil's voice drifts down.

We all look up and see him crouching on the top of the wall, peering over it at us.

"You've been listening in?" Drosdan hisses.

Samil's scales tint with shades of shame as he nods.

"Right," Drosdan says, hands balling into fists. "You go to

the City. Report to Visidion and Rosalind then get back here with their input."

"Got it," Samil says.

He disappears from sight, and in a moment, we hear his feet hitting the sand on the far side of the wall.

"Put him to some use," I say, shaking my head.

"He's a strange one," Drosdan sighs. "Hardly a male."

Nodding and silent agreement from the circle, then we disperse to our duties. As I walk towards my forge, I notice several of the females are standing in the main cave, looking out towards us. Heat flashes across my scales, my tail stiffens, and my hands close into fists, angry at the sight. The bijass rages, vying for control.

How can they be so ignorant? These females are head-strong and put themselves in danger as if it's the way their lives should be led. If they would only listen!

Storming to the cave I fully intend to give them a solid berating. How are we to protect them when they won't follow the most basic tenets of safety?

Before I open my mouth, I feel her. Then an instant later, I see her. She steps out of the darkness of the cave, concern in her eyes, her skin wan and waxy.

"What's happened?" she asks, a quiver to her voice

The anger is gone, instantly—when I set eyes on her, there is nothing left of it.

"It's nothing, go inside, all of you," I say, motioning with my arms.

"We want to know," Olivia says, stepping forward, defiant.

The anger rolls out again like thunderclouds, but Maeve places a hand on my arm, and the suns come out.

"I'll tell you, go in, where it's safe," I say, gazing at her hand resting on mine.

Warmth flows from her touch. My scales tingle, and the first hints of arousal stir in my cock.

I follow the females into the cave, ushering them along until they're deep enough, and the only light is from the candles dotting the walls and work tables.

"The miners believe that the Invaders are collecting meteorite glass," I say.

"What? Why?" a chorus of questions echoes off the stone walls, too fast and too many for me to answer.

I wait for it to end, staring at them while their rapid-fire talk bounces off of me. Maeve, for her part, stands silent, waiting. Pride wells in my stomach, sending tingles out along my arms and legs.

When they finish speaking and are all staring at me, I continue.

"We don't know," I say. "It does mean that we're going to keep tight security. Don't go out in the open alone. Always have a Zmaj with you."

"But if they want the glass, do we let them have it?" Bailey asks.

"No," I say, shaking my head. "Zmaj do not give ground to our enemies."

"How? What are we going to do to stop them?" Penelope asks.

"Gather it first," I answer, simple and direct.

"You said we're not to go outside," someone says, but I miss who spoke.

"Right," I say. "We'll do it. The males."

A mutter runs through the females. I look from one to another, and I don't understand why they're muttering in discontent. It is the most logical thing. We are the warriors—why would it be anyone but us to risk ourselves? Our duty is to protect them. They are female.

The muttering stops, and Maeve steps closer. She places a hand on my arm, her brilliant eyes boring into me. Warmth spreads across my scales where she touches, the embedded meteorite glass pulses with life of its own, accenting her touch.

"Padraig," she says, her voice soft but insistent. "You can't be this way. Please."

"Be this way?" I ask, tilting my head to one side.

The world fades away around us, we might as well be alone. She is all, the center of the universe.

"Yes," she says. "We are not frail, incapable things, we can help."

"You are female," I reply.

"Yes," she agrees. "We are. That doesn't mean we are incapable."

Confusion is a spinning mess inside my thoughts. Of course they are not incapable, they're female. How can she not understand her role?

Yes, there are exceptions, Lana drifts through my thoughts but I will not have my female be a hunter. Ragnar, well he does what he does. That is between him and his mate. It is not my business to set him straight.

"You are female," I say again, pushing my one thought.

"We've more than established that," she says, shaking her head then she sighs.

"It is my duty, my honor, to keep you safe," tearing my eyes from hers I look at the assembled humans. "All of you."

"Right," she says, disappointment so heavy in her voice that an ache forms in my chest.

"We'll talk later," she says, turning away and rejoining the others.

"Good," I say, feeling as if I've won a hollow victory.

Turning away, I leave, hearing them move deeper into the cave, which is all I wanted in the first place. Safety, why do they protest against being cared for?

Females do not make sense, but they are what they are.

Perhaps they're not supposed to? Is this the fate of all matings?

Taking up my hammer, I beat out my upsets and anger on the steel I'm forming to reinforce the gate.

Time passes, my focus in full on the work to hand. It's a relief to push aside the questions I don't have answers to or any way to resolve.

The suns are dropping low when I bother to look around again. The day has passed, and while I've made significant progress on improving the gate, I'm no closer to an answer about Maeve.

After scooping ash from a bucket, I cover the coals of the forge so that they will be ready to come to life in the morning, I head towards dinner.

The communal tables have all been moved inside the main cavern for safety. Before I step into the cave, Maeve pushes off the side wall and stops me.

"We need to talk," she says.

"Yes," I agree, but my stomach grumbles loudly. I've worked right through lunch.

"Come with me," she says.

She starts up the ramp and goes towards my room. She pulls the heavy leather door aside and motions I should go in, so I do, allowing her to keep the lead.

She closes the door behind us, and then she is in my arms, hers wrapped around me, holding me tight.

"You're impossible," she says into my chest.

Closing my arms around her, I don't understand what she is doing, but more than anything, I don't care. She is in my arms, and that is all I need.

We hold each other for a while in silence. I massage the muscles of her back. It's not uncomfortable, though I do have the sensation there is more to come that I don't expect to be nearly so good.

When she raises her head off my chest and looks up to me, I lean down to kiss her, but she pulls back, denying me. My heart sinks, and I know this is where it goes bad.

Words.

Ugh, why can she not be malleable like the steel I forged today?

"Padraig," she says. "You can't treat us like you have been. You have to be better."

"Better?" I ask.

If I stick to single words, maybe I'll be able to make her understand.

"Yes!" she exclaims, pushing off of me fully and placing her hands on her hips. "We're not delicate flowers. You don't have to— No, you *can't* protect us all the time."

"Can't I?"

"No! Wait, yes, you can, but not the way you are," she says, shaking her head and sounding more upset.

"How?" I ask.

I'm genuinely curious. I don't know how else to do what needs to be done. Protecting them is the only thing, without them there is no future. I will not return to the way things were before they came. That is something I can't face.

She stares, her face blank, lips pursed, eyes wide. Her mouth opens, then snaps shut.

The fullness of her lips calls to me, and my desire arises despite the gravity of the conversation. She is so beautiful, so perfect. I know she's angry with me, but even in anger she is gorgeous.

"You respect us!" she says, her voice rising.

"I do," I say, shaking my head in confusion. "How can I help but? You are... everything."

She starts to say more but my words stop her. Our eyes lock. We're drawn together, as if by an outside force, the connection between us pulsing with a life of its own. She trembles, her lips quivering, and moisture wells in the corners of her eyes.

"Everything?" she asks, her voice hardly a whisper.

My throat is too tight for words, my hearts have jumped into it, so I nod.

She is all. All I can do is let the overwhelming emotion I feel pour out of me, flowing towards her, and hope beyond hope that she understands. How else can I make this real to her?

She falls into my arms, and I sweep her up off her feet. The soft, fresh scent of her hair fills my nostrils as I crush her against my chest.

Hands roaming down her back, I hook under her ass and she wraps her legs around my waist. Our lips meet, and she drives her tongue into my mouth. She is taking me, claiming my mouth as hers.

My cock aches, throbbing between my legs, straining to be free. A sense of desperation enhances our desire. I have to have her and the same is obvious in her. Hands scrambling over each other, clothing flies around the room until at last we're naked, exposed to each other.

Our lips barely part as we tear the cloth from each other's bodies. Her hands twine in my hair, pulling, forcing my head back.

Roughly she kisses my neck and behind my ear, her lips sucking as she moves down towards my shoulder.

She shifts her position, pulling herself up. With my erect dick sticking straight out, she lowers herself so she's sitting on top of it.

Groaning, I try to lift her, wanting to be inside of her, but she jerks on my hair, stopping me. She shifts her hips back and forth so her wetness coats the top side of my cock.

It's a new sensation, intense in its pleasure.

She gasps when her pelvis meets mine, and I'm sure the

hard ridge has met her clit. That's its purpose after all, giving the female pleasure.

She pulls up and down, then she slides back along my shaft and slowly forward.

With her hair grasped in one hand, I take my turn to pull her head back and kiss along her neck to her delicate, perfect shoulder. She gasps and groans.

Tightness builds in my balls and stomach. The urge to explode keeps climbing, until it takes all my concentration not to.

She continues the motion, faster now, groaning louder, matching my own exclamations of pleasure.

She grabs my face between her hands and stares into my eyes. She bites her lower lip, the lids of her eyes dropping to half-closed.

"I'm going to come," she whispers.

Shifting my hands back to under her ass, I support her loosely, protecting her as she gives herself over to her pleasure. Leaning back against the wall, I feel my own point of no return, dancing on that edge. Holding back until her satisfaction is achieved.

"Yes, yes, yes," she says, exhaling heavily with each syllable.

Her body moves faster, increasing the tempo. Watching her pleasure build creates a sense of euphoria in me that is more than any simple release of fluid.

The raging inferno of emotions that she creates consumes my body. Pulling memories and all that I am in as fuel. Blasting me with its fiery heat.

"Yes!" she cries out.

Her back arches as her hands tighten on my face, then scrabbling, she has my hair and is jerking it over and over as her orgasm grips her body.

I hold her tight yet gentle, supporting her release as it

rages through. Watching her body spasm, her full breasts shaking with the force of it.

I try to hold back but watching her is too much. My cock explodes, spewing its seed out onto the floor. Jumping over and over as it drains my first load.

At last she collapses in my arms, her head on my shoulder, her arms encircling my neck.

I hold her silently, not moving or shifting a muscle, giving her time to recover. She breathes heavily. The echo of her heart pounds in the back of my head.

It slows from a gallop towards a normal rhythm, and at last she raises her head. Her soft, full lips find mine, kissing gently. Softly she grabs my lower lip between her teeth and tugs, giggling as she does.

I lick her upper lip, and she shifts her bottom, pulling herself up. My second cock has risen to the occasion, and in moments she is lowering herself onto it.

Her wet warmth engulfs my dick greedily. The moment I push into her, relief washes through me.

It's transcending the physical. When I join with her, electrical pulses race through my body, warm, tingling. I'm losing myself in her. Her warmth takes me, claiming me for her own.

"Padraig," she gasps, jerking my hair.

I turn us around so I can press her against the wall, allowing me to push deeper into her.

Burying my cock deep in her eager pussy, I'm accepted into her fully. Impaled on me and pressed to the wall, she is mine.

Finding her mouth, I force my tongue past her soft, pliable lips. She greets it with her own, wrestling with mine. When she moans into the kiss, her sweet breath fills my mouth.

I drive into her, over and over. Taking my pleasure while giving her hers. It's what we both need now.

She groans, I groan, the sounds of our love fill the small space of the room.

I'm changing, awakening something inside of both of us. We're changing in ways I don't understand, but the sensations carry us along on a river.

Our journey is far from over. Dim memories surge out of the fog of the bijass as I push in and out of her.

I was lost. Buried alive, left for dead. Long forgotten, I'd let the fog of the bijass claim that piece of me, but now it returns, at this worst possible moment. I don't want that memory, so I focus on her.

Her bright eyes, the way she bites her lip, the way her cheeks suck in and out. She throws her head back, thrusting her hips into mine, forcing me deeper into her.

It doesn't matter.

The future is ours. She is the future. I know, without shadow of doubt, with her beside me, we can create something extraordinary. It is our destiny, our fate.

My dragon hums its pleasure, and a low growl slips out as the excitement increases.

She is mine.

"Maeve," I growl her name, pushing in deep and holding her.

Her eyes roll up into her head as she throws it back and cries out.

Squeezing her ass, I pull her tight against me. My second cock releases its seed into her.

Her body takes it greedily, drinking my dick dry. My balls spasm as the last load pushes out until I have nothing left to give. Resting My head against the wall I hold her impaled on my cock, letting the spasms of our pleasure pass.

She clings to my neck, her body shaking until the final

vestiges of her orgasm fade away.

Only after several moments have passed do I lift her off my softening cock and lower her to the floor. She tries to stand but her knees must be weak for she starts to fall, laughing.

"Oh wow," she says as I catch and hold her.

Once she is on her feet, I let her go. She wavers a moment, and I stand ready to catch her if she needs it. She holds out a hand then steadies, nodding. She looks up, her eyes alight with delight.

"Damn," she says, shaking her head.

I put my hands on the wall and pin her in once more, leaning in and stealing kisses from her soft lips. She trails her fingers across my chest, tracing the lines of my scales. Energy courses between us, exchanging, intertwining. It doesn't make sense, isn't something I can put into words, but it's real and it's there.

She's gravity pulling me. There is no escape from her, but I don't want to go anywhere. She nibbles my lower lip, just hard enough to feel it, and my first cock starts to rise again. My devotion to her is absolute. I am hers.

The pulsing electrical force flowing between us enhances every sensation. Her touch is all I crave, sensation overload that overwhelms my senses.

She grabs my rising cock and strokes it roughly. It's bold, forward, and absolutely erotic. My dick is hard as a rock and ready for her instantly. We go again.

I lift her off her feet and carry her to the bed without breaking our kiss.

As I lower her onto it, she spreads her legs, welcoming me. Immediately I thrust in, seating myself fully inside of her. We thrust in time with each other, letting the sensations build, slow but sure.

She grips my hips with her legs, rising up onto her elbows

and looks into my eyes.

"Roll over," she orders.

Carefully keeping myself inside of her I do as she asks. On top of me, she puts her arms behind her head and pulls her hair up. Her exposed breasts, so incredibly erotic in any situation, jut out before her, rising and pulling tight against her body.

I grab them both, encasing them in my hands, rubbing the tips with my thumbs.

She groans, rotating her hips. The sensation as she swirls around on my cock is intense, and I have to concentrate to not lose control.

"Yes," she hisses, biting her lips, her eyes closed as she rises and falls on my dick.

Sliding my hands down to her waist I lift her up and down, helping her with the push and pull of our lovemaking. I'm building fast to yet another release when the ground beneath us rumbles.

"Yes!" she cries out loudly, thrusting harder but I stop.

She doesn't. Moving a hand to her mouth, I cover it over, wrapping my free arm around her waist and holding her still.

The rumble repeats. This time it makes jars rattle on a small shelf.

Her eyes widen, and she nods. I take my hand off her mouth. Slowly, trying to make no noise, she climbs off of my dick.

"Zemlja?" she mouths the word.

Placing my fingertips on the hard floor I close my eyes and concentrate. It doesn't feel right so I shake my head no. I do put a finger over my lips, but only to be safe. No need to make extra noise in case I'm wrong.

Maeve nods, and I climb to my feet, put my pants on, and then go to the door. The soft whisper of cloth behind me says Maeve is also dressing in an efficient and quiet manner.

"There!" Arawn yells as soon as I open the door.

He's on the wall, yelling and pointing up. Following the indication, I look up too. Six of the Invader ships fly overhead.

Six of them.

My heart sinks. If they attack now, there is no way our faulty shield will hold.

Instinctively, I grab Maeve around her waist and pull her out the door with me. The main cave will be the only chance. I have to get her into it now.

"Wha—" she starts but is cut off as I pull her out the door.

Lifting her off her feet I carry her in one arm and run towards the main cave. She's smart enough to not resist as I race. Single-minded focus pulling me to the best safety I have for her.

As I step into the shadow of the opening, I set her on her feet and glance back up at the sky. The last of the ships has passed over. They haven't started firing, yet.

My hearts pound hard and my breath is rapid. Tingles run along my scales as I scan the sky, searching.

Nothing.

"They're headed for the City!" Ragnar's voice drifts across the open area.

"No," I say, shaking my head.

Ragnar, Melchior, Arawn, and Drosdan all run up to the main cave coming from different directions.

"The City?" I ask.

Samil runs up, panting.

"Yes," Samil says, "I ran out onto the dunes, they're making right for it."

Drosdan harrumphs, shaking his head.

"Will the dome hold?" Melchior asks.

"There are not many Zmaj in the City," Ragnar says. "They'll need help if they break through."

"We can't all go," Arawn adds.

"We can't not go," I say, an empty pit in my stomach at the thought of leaving Maeve behind, but I can't take her into battle.

"Right," Drosdan says. "Visidion is there. We have to send help, in case they need it, if nothing else."

"Who stays?" Ragnar asks.

"I'll stay with the Elders, Samil with me," Drosdan says. "Ragnar, Melchior, Arawn, Padraig all go. Now."

I nod and look back at Maeve. Her face is pale, her eyes wide, but she opens her mouth, then snaps it shut.

"Go," she whispers, nodding.

I meet her eyes but all I have time to do is return her nod. I run to my room, grab my lochaber and pack, and meet the others at the gate.

Running across the sand towards the City, unhindered by the need to slow for humans, we make excellent time. In the distance I can see the Invader ships racing towards the city, outlined by the light of the night sky.

None of us speak. There's no need. We know what has to be done. The journey to the City is long, but we have no time to waste if we're going to make it in time to help.

The moon shifts across the sky as we run. I'm tireless. I don't know where I'm pulling energy from. It's been a long day of hard labor, followed by my time with Maeve, yet none of that slows me.

My thoughts are, as usual, on Maeve. We haven't said words describing what we are yet, and I know that the humans don't see things the same as Zmaj. Mating alone does not mean, to them, for life.

It's something that I need to talk about with her and I know it. As I run, I think of different ways I could bring it up, and how she might respond, playing out scenarios in my mind's eye.

It has to be done right. It may not be forever in her mind, but I know it will be once she understands. It's the same with the other females that have mated with Zmaj. They are solid pairs now. Coupled, mated for life, but it wasn't easy for them either. They had to work for it.

I will work for her. I will kill for her. I will do anything for her.

The depth of emotion that swells inside of me is a thing of its own. Powerful, almost to the point of being frightening. I've never felt this way about anyone or anything.

If I can't have Maeve...

No, it's not an option. There is no world I want anything to do with unless she is in it.

The fog of the bijass surges in and out, dancing around the edges of thought as I consider. Suddenly it spits out a memory, and I stumble in my running.

Suffocating. Trapped, can't move.

No, that's the memory. It's not now—it's not real.

Pushing past the immediacy of the memory, I'm able to focus my thoughts again in the now. It takes a moment, but I manage it.

Ragnar and Arawn both look over in concern. I shake my head indicating it's nothing, and we all run on in silence.

The memory doesn't fade even as I'm able to push it away from consuming my thoughts. It's no longer the now, but it's strong, here again.

During the Devastation I was trapped, buried alive and left for dead in a mine.

Cold chills race across my scales. I'd given this memory to the bijass and never wanted to see it again. The sound of my brethren, my fellow gatherers deciding to leave me. Running in fear as the walls of the cave we were in collapsed.

Betrayed.

They all betray you in the end. No one will stand with

you, and when it's time to die, you die alone.

Emptiness pounds through me, trying to absorb me. A blackness that threatens to soak up my thoughts.

Maeve. Desperate to maintain control, I turn to her. My treasure, my rock, the one I know is meant for me.

My deepest nature, my dragon, roars to life, and the pain of the memory burns in its ire.

She will not abandon me. Yes, there is much to discuss, but it doesn't matter. In the end, we are meant one for another. That is what will happen.

Ragnar skids to a stop. I run a few steps past him before it registers, and I stop too.

"No!" he hisses, pointing up to the sky.

Two of the Invader ships race back towards us. Towards the Tribe.

My hearts stop. Can't breathe. They're heading for Maeve!

I'm running, not bothering with words, heading for her. I have to save her.

"Arawn, Melchior, go to the City, we'll go back," he barks.

His mate is back there too. In moments he's beside me again, and we both pour all we can into our run. I glance over without stopping.

"We'll make it," he says, certainty in his eyes and his voice unquavering. "They'll be fine."

"They must be," I say.

"Good choice, Brother," he says.

It cuts through the chaos of my thoughts. I look at him fully for the first time, and he smiles.

"You think we wouldn't notice?" he asks, shaking his head. "It's about time someone took that chip off your shoulder, as the humans say."

I don't have any words to answer him with, so I nod and we continue running.

9

MAEVE

I've been trying to distract myself with thoughts of our future, planning the layout of our future cave, remembering song lyrics, but it's not working. His hearts beat steadily in the back of my thoughts. I know he's okay, for right now, but that's the problem. It's for right now.

His heartbeat is like thunder inside my body now, enough to rock me back and forth, just a tiny bit. I'm so grateful for it. In a way. Because what would I do if it stopped?

That was a lot of ships flying overhead. When they reach the City...

"Stop!" Delilah exclaims, placing her hand over mine. "Please, enough."

"What," I say, "Was I doing it again?"

"You were moving the whole table," Delilah says. "Stop drumming your fingers!"

"Sorry," I say, unable to meet her eyes.

"She's worried," Penelope says. "We all are."

"Yes," Delilah agrees. "Let's not get on each other's nerves, how about that?"

"I said sorry," I say, irritation rising.

"I know," she says, patting my hand. "It's fine. We're all on edge."

No one says any more. We've all gathered at the communal dinner table. There's a low buzz of conversation, but it's stilted and forced. No one can keep one going for long before they stop and listen—as if that's going to tell us anything.

Drosdan, Samil, Ryuth, Kalessin and several of the other Zmaj stand near the cave entrance, staring out into the dark night.

Zmaj night vision is better by far than a human's but they're not talking, not even to each other. The rest of the Zmaj of the Tribe aren't in sight, but I know they're out there, ready for anything.

It doesn't change what I want. Padraig. Here, with me.

How can I be feeling for him what I do? He's not the type of man I dreamed of or ever thought I would end up being with, but I can't deny my emotions.

I've never been that close with anyone. Delilah is probably my best friend, and she doesn't know much about me either. I know more of her life than she does mine. I've never been open to sharing much, but with him...

Ugh, how can I feel this way about anyone? I want to share everything with him. I want to know everything about him. He's so different.

He's changing.

For me.

He's changing for me.

What human man would ever do that? Sure, in the great romance stories men change for their love, but in real life? Yeah, right. Men are men, they are what they are, and they don't really change that.

Or so I thought. No, so I saw happen. All the men on the ship were what they were, and that was the story of it. You had to find one that you liked as they were because if you didn't you were going to be miserable.

We all had a duty to make babies and such but there weren't any prearranged marriages, or if there were, they weren't common. I never heard of one.

My life on the ship was tough. My mom was in an accident and in a coma when I was five years old. After that I was raised by nurses and passed around a lot. I watched a movie once about a red-headed orphan who sang a song about tomorrow. It was cute, and when I was a kid, I really identified with her.

I wasn't really unwanted, but then I wasn't really wanted either. I was a duty, not a desire.

I think my Mom felt differently. I kind of remember it being so, but those memories are so dim, I'm not sure about that either. It wasn't bad, but then it wasn't great either. I guess it made me tough, so there's that.

Really, I never had anyone I could trust. My 'parents' changed regularly. I moved from home to home based on the whims of fate and chance. If one set of parents got tired of me, had to work more, or had a kid of their own come along, I was shuffled to the next one.

They were all nice. I wasn't abused or mistreated or anything, but there was no stability. I didn't make friends at school, because at any moment I'd change schools and lose the ones I made. I learned that after the third time. It hurt so much to leave my friends, I decided I wasn't going to do it anymore.

Now here I am, and this jerk of an alien-dragon man comes traipsing in, gets past all my walls and defenses, and sets up camp in my heart.

What the hell twist of fate is this?

Strange but I can't deny it.

I care too much about him. If I didn't why am I so afraid he won't come back?

"We should do something," Penelope says.

"Sure," I agree, hoping for anything that will take me out of my own thoughts.

"We could try to plan out the Christmas thing," Delilah offers.

"Yeah!" Penelope agrees.

Shaking my head, I smile and shrug. That's not the kind of thing I was hoping to have for a distraction, but it's better than nothing.

"So, we should set up some guidelines on it," Penelope says. "I was thinking if we made the gifts gender neutral then we could put them all in a pile and everyone could pick one. That would make it more exciting."

"What if you want to give your gift to a specific person?" Delilah asks.

"Well that wouldn't work if we did that," Penelope says. "It would ruin the entire idea. It's supposed to be about the giving and the surprise of not knowing who's going to get your gift is fun."

"Sure, I love it when I get ceramic elephants," Delilah says sourly.

"Oh, come on," Penelope says.

"I like it," I throw in.

The ground rumbles beneath us, and silence falls instantly. A learned reaction that you pick up fast on Tajss if you want to live. Everyone knows that the zemlja hunt by sound.

It rumbles harder and now it's not difficult at all to tell that it's not a zemlja. The ships are coming back.

"No," I gasp.

All of us at the table look at each other, eyes wide with fear. I run to the cave opening. The Zmaj stationed there have left. When I get there and look out, I see why.

Two of the ships hover overhead, and one is landing outside the wall. The Zmaj are racing to engage the Invaders.

My heart leaps into my throat.

Cold ice forms a knot in my stomach. This can't be— they're here too. In the back of my head the soft thrumming that has become almost normal doubles up. Something is happening with Padraig too.

"No," I say, my voice barely a whisper.

The shield is up but it's flickering. I don't know how long it will last if they start firing. The Zmaj have their weapons out and are racing through the gate to engage those outside the wall.

Overhead a ship hovers but it's not firing, not yet. I have to help, somehow. I'm scanning the area, the hair on my arms standing on end, looking for something, anything I can do to help. I can't sit back cowering while the Zmaj risk themselves.

"We have to help," Delilah says, gripping my arm tight.

"Right, but not be stupid," I say.

"Right." She's looking too.

"We don't have enough glass to power the shield," she says.

"Okay, let's fix that," I say, laying my hand over hers.

We lock eyes, and it's clear we both know that this is stupid. Beyond stupid, but it's also our one hope. The Zmaj are probably enough to handle the Invaders outside the wall, but if the shield comes down, then we'll either be blasted by the ships above, or overwhelmed because they can drop right in on us.

Taking a deep breath, we nod as one, turn, and run for the machine under Errol's work space.

As soon as we step out into the open my fear triples. Sweat pours into my eyes, my heart races, and the hair on back of my neck is straight up. There's an itchy sensation as if at any moment I'm going to be hit from behind.

We run flat out, heads down, arms and legs pumping. We're about halfway when the first blast hits the shield. Delilah yelps as loudly as I do, making me feel better. I nearly jump out of my skin when it hits. It's a loud explosion followed by a crackling sound as the electrical bolt races across the surface of the shield.

Sliding across the dirt we come to a halt under the canopy of Errol's workshop.

The machine whines, a high-pitched cry making it clear we're in trouble. A basket of meteorite glass sits next to it ready to be used but it's not enough.

"Do we have any more?" I ask.

"I don't think so," Delilah says, leaping to the basket and handing pieces to me.

I feed them into the machine but it's burning through them. Another explosion lights up the night as the ship fires again. This is bad.

"Okay," I say, wiping sweat away from my eyes.

My mind is racing as fast as my heart is beating. It hurts to breathe. It's so intense. Looking around, desperate, I spot more glass by the wall, close to the open gate.

The Zmaj on the far side of the gate are engaged with the Invaders. The ringing of steel on steel, the fire of energy weapons that seem to do nothing to slow the Zmaj.

The glass is close to the Invaders who outnumber the Zmaj at least four to one. No matter how impressive, no, how downright amazing they are in battle, the numbers are against them.

Going closer to the Invaders isn't smart. Could be considered stupid by any rational person. Debate rages for only a moment when the ship above fires and the dome flickers. Delilah and I look at each other, and she must see it on my face for her eyes widen, her mouth drops open.

"Maeve!" she screams but I'm away, her words coming past my back.

Stupid, stupid, stupid, I chant in my head over and over as I run.

Have to make it, almost there.

Another explosion, the night sky lights up bright as day, and there's a sickening sound of electricity crackling through the air.

"RUN!" Delilah's voice drifts along with the sound of the exploding guns overhead.

The battle outside the wall is louder here. Steel clashing with steel ringing in my ears. The explosions, the ringing, is deafening.

My awareness contracts down to the tunnel between me and that basket full of glass. I have to reach it, move faster!

Screaming at my legs to go, I try to will myself to move quicker. I throw on the brakes when I reach the wall, then grab the basket and lift, turning back to Delilah.

It's heavy, much heavier than I expected. My muscles scream as I hoist it up to my hip, leaning to the side to balance the extra weight.

I can't quite run, not fully. It's a quick shuffle but I'm doing my best. One foot in front of another, move, girl, move! The fire explodes overhead once more, lighting the world up bright. It's bright enough to see Delilah's eyes widen, her mouth open, and she reaches an arm out towards me, all before the sound of her scream reaches my ears.

Her scream and the cold hand that grabs me by my

shoulder happen at once. I'm spun around, the basket of glass flying off my hip and spilling across the packed sand.

I'm lifted off my feet by my shoulder. There's searing pain as my captor shakes my body like it's nothing, lifting me up before its helmeted face.

The helmet is dark, so I can't see the creature behind it. It holds me up, inspecting me as if I'm an interesting insect. A section over what must be its eyes clears and I see depthless black orbs staring out at me with cold intention.

"What do you want!" I scream, kicking at it ineffectively.

"Everything," it says, its voice a nasty gurgling sound. "All of this is ours to take."

My blood runs cold. The evil in its voice, more than its words, strikes fear into my heart. My side burns, and a red glow shines from the meteorite glass embedded in my ribs. The alien's eyes drop to it, widening in surprise. As it lifts me higher to look at the glass, I stop struggling. It inspects the glass with those cold, empty eyes, then I smile.

"Screw you," I spit in its face, and kick with all I have.

Swinging loosely in its grip, my kick carries me forward and lands squarely in his crotch. Pain explodes in my foot, and I'm sure it's broken.

As I cry out, another explosion hits the shield overhead. The light doesn't reach us. a shadow stops it.

"MAEVE!" Padraig screams.

His wings block the bright light from overhead. His lochaber flashes as he swings it through the air and cleaves the monster holding me.

As I tumble to the ground, blood and gore spray across me. I try to roll, but it's a graceless fall. I hit hard, my head bounces, and the wind is knocked out of me.

An instant after impact, I'm in his arms. He holds me, gentle, yet firm against his chest.

"Maeve!" his deep, rumbling voice cracks on my name.

I move my mouth, struggling to speak and gasp in the desperately needed air. My eyes water, my lungs burn, and the world takes on a gray overcast.

No! I can't pass out. I won't give in.

"Yes," I hiss, a thin stream of air leaking into my lungs at last.

His eyes bore into mine, his hands move over my body, but he doesn't wait for more. He's running, and I'm bouncing against him.

"Take her, care for her," he barks. "Let nothing happen to her."

"I've got her," Lana says, as he dumps me into her arms.

When I turn my head to see him, everything hurts, but worse is the ache in my chest as he races out to battle. I don't want to say it, give voice to the feelings that continue to grow in my heart. I'm falling for him.

How, why, I don't know, but I am. Saying anything else is a lie. He's a misunderstood warrior, and I know, beyond the shadow of any doubt, he'll do anything for me.

"Let me look at you," Delilah says, hooking my arm over her shoulders.

She helps me limp further into the cavern and sets me into a chair. The throbbing pain in my foot is the worst, but it's not all for sure. Every part of my body hurts, to one degree or another.

"Are they going to be okay?" I ask, tears falling.

It's more than the pain, it's fear. Fear I won't see him again. Fear he'll be hurt defending us.

"They'll be fine," she says, the smallest of tremors in her voice. "They have to be."

She mutters the last as she runs her hands down my sides.

"Ah!" I exclaim, jerking away when her hand passes over my left side.

"There?" she asks, looking up for confirmation.

"Yeah, there, and there . . . and around there," I add, pointing to other points of pain.

"You're an idiot," she says, shaking her head.

"Yeah," I agree. "I had to try."

"I know," she sighs, heavily.

The sounds of battle echo distantly. It's dim here in the cavern. Almost a background noise, like something you might play to go to sleep. A constant clashing dissonance, but somehow it seems natural.

"Delilah," I whisper.

"Yeah?" she asks, working on removing my shoe.

I'll take pride in the fact I only cry out once as she pulls it off. My foot is black and blue and already swelling.

"I'm scared," I say, not raising my voice.

"Me too," she agrees, looking at my foot.

"I don't think it's broke," she says, running her fingers softly along it. "Can't be sure, but you sure as heck bruised it, sprained, most likely."

"Okay," I say, resting my head against the wall.

"I'll wrap it up," she says, rising to get bandages.

"Thanks," I say, closing my eyes to focus on the sounds of the battle outside.

"It was impressive," Delilah says.

When I open my eyes, she's looking at me, her eyes alight with silent laughter.

"Yeah?" I ask.

"Oh yeah, you probably didn't see the look on that thing's face when you kicked him in the nards," she laughs. "Priceless."

"The alien has nards," I laugh, but it hurts. "Ooh!" Grabbing my ribs, I hold them and cut off the laughter.

"Be careful," Delilah admonishes.

"Got that," I agree. "Now."

Over the din of battle comes a long, low rumbling cry,

and I instantly recognize Padraig's voice. Deep, grinding, beautiful, and sexy as he fights for me.

For all of us, but I know, by the beating of his hearts in my head, he fights for me above all.

I'm a fool. A fool for him, but a fool. This can't be good, but if it isn't, why does it feel so damn right?

10

PADRAIG

*R*age. Red covers my vision. The bijass grips me fully and I embrace it. Slash, cut, dodge, jump, one action leading to the next.

My pain is distant, barely registering past the red fog. The old tales from long before the Devastation told of Zmaj warriors and their glory in battle, but they did not tell of their pain. It means nothing to me.

Maeve is hurt.

These monsters did it.

They will feel my wrath.

They will know pain.

They will die.

No one hurts my treasure. No one touches my treasure. No one.

One of the monster's fires, electrical energy, bursts on my chest, crawling along my scales with blue lightning. It hurts, tingles, and makes the muscles of my arms feel numb.

The burning fire of my anger pushes it aside, feeds on it, and takes the pain and agony as fuel to burn hotter. I lower my lochaber and leap forward, wings spreading to catch air, land in front of the Invader, and grab him by his throat.

After lifting him off the ground, I hold him over my head and shake. The sound of his neck snapping, heard even through his armor, is music to my ears. I throw his lifeless body at two more who approach, throwing off their aim before they can fire their weapons.

I'm on them before they recover, my blade singing through the air and slicing through them as easily as I'd slice through a piece of soft leather.

One to another. The song of battle whistles through my body, calls to my soul, but behind it all is a single, steady beating sound. One rhythm that makes it all matter. Her.

Her heart thrums in the back of my head, hammering with her fear and her pain. Giving meaning to every motion I make. Reason to fight, and more than that, reason to be victorious.

Dimly, I'm aware of my brethren. On some level, I feel them too, but it's nothing compared to the way I can feel her. I'm ahead of them, too far, out on my own.

I stop and turn in a circle. I'm surrounded. Eight Invaders encircle me, two of them have an electrified net, while the others have a mix of swords and guns.

"Take him," one of them yells, his voice guttural and cold.

"Bring it," I smile, throwing my arms wide in welcome.

This is what a male lives for, to pit himself against impossible odds, but I am Zmaj. No odds are impossible to me. I will be victorious!

"Ahhh!" I cry out, letting my rage out in a single, wordless cry.

They close in, stabbing with their swords. Three stand back, firing repeatedly with their guns. Blue electricity crackles from the weapons, and the impact of each shot delivers numbing force to my scales.

Feinting to the left, I shift and move right, grabbing one of the swordsmen with the fake out.

Pulling him to my chest I hold him by his neck, using his body as a shield against the guns.

I'm still taking hits from behind, but I turn a circle as fast as I can, trying to slow them down. The pain is enough that it's reading past the bijass.

A net flies through the air. If I don't move, I'll be entangled.

Letting my prisoner go, I duck and then roll, but I don't stop until I slam into one of the gunmen.

He grunts, bringing his gun down to bear, but I leap up, slamming my head under his chin. A vulnerable spot in his armor.

His head snaps back with a crack, then he drops.

I don't take time to rest. Leaping, I flap my wings to get air and put distance between myself and the group. Even the best warrior knows that one against many is foolish odds. I'm not a fool.

After landing, I spin on my heel to face them.

They're in confusion as they turn to face me. Random shots fire but go wide. Shifting my grip on my lochaber, I throw it like a spear. It slams into the second gun wielder, leaving only one standing.

The one with a net swirls it in one hand, preparing to throw, while the remaining men with swords spread out, trying to flank me again.

I back up slowly, keeping them all in my lines of sight, letting them make the first move.

A man to my left moves, then the one to the right does too, closing in with swords swinging high. A heart's beat, then another and I duck and roll forward, moving between them. Kicking out as I roll past them, my foot connects with the net wielder. The shin of his leg cracks, and he drops to the ground screaming in pain.

I jump up, slam a foot into his face, cracking his helmet and silencing his cries of pain.

I wrench my lochaber from the chest of one monster and turn to face the others. I smile.

The scent of their fear taints the air and the thrill of battle awakens inside of me. The dragon roars in delight.

Conquest, protection, my treasure will be safe.

Fear creates hesitation, for them, but not for me. It's the only edge I need. Moving as fast as I can, I close with them, blade slicing and dicing, and in only a few beats of my hearts, they're down.

"MAEVE!" I roar her name as my victory cry.

My treasure will know that her male is strong and able to protect her from all threats.

With red fog covering my vision, I search for the next threat. The ground rumbles as a roar fills the sky. The ships overhead dart away. The one that had landed lifts off and joins their retreat. All of us roar as one, victory!

My brethren come close. We stare at one another, each of us struggling with our bijass. The red haze demanding that one of us be dominant.

Drosdan steps into the middle of the circle.

Take him. Dominate.

"I am myself," he intones, hands unclenching, arms hanging at his side.

"Together we are stronger," a few voices join him.

The bijass claws at my thoughts as I assert myself over it. Primal instinct raging, I am the dominant one. I should be in control.

Maeve's sweet lips form in my mind's eye, and as it pulls back, I see her face.

The red fog retreats.

"Survival of the Tribe matters," I intone with the rest.

We close with one another, clasping arms and embracing. Under control again, we return to the caves.

Pain comes as the bijass retreats. The rush of battle held it at bay, but now I'm very much aware of the beating I put my body through.

When we pass through the wall, the females run out of the cave towards us. My eyes lock on Maeve, and my heart soars.

"Padraig!" she yells, her voice cracking as she limps towards me.

Anger rips through me when I see her bandaged foot, but it can't compete with my joy at the sight of her. I've defeated all who would harm her. She is mine. My greatest treasure is safe.

I run to her, limping myself as various parts of my body protest the fast movement, and I sweep her into my arms. Smashing my lips into hers, I spin her around, squeezing her tight against me.

"Are you okay?" I ask, holding her out at arm's length, so I can look her up and down.

"Yes," she says, wetness streaming from her eyes. "You're hurt."

"I'm fine," I say. "You are all that matters."

The smile on her face, the light in her eyes, the sound of her heart in my head racing all create a sensation of expansion and joy unlike anything I've experienced.

It's overwhelming. My throat closes, and it feels like both of my hearts are in it pounding as they try to leap out of my mouth to give themselves to her.

"You matter," she says, shaking her head. "Put me down so I can look you over."

Obeying her order, I set her back on her feet and she

limps closer. She inspects my body, tsking and sighing as she looks over the damage.

"I'm fine," I argue, but she shushes me until she's done her own thorough inspection.

"Most of the blood isn't yours, thankfully," she says.

"Our enemies," I say, nodding.

"Right, but it's more than we have water supply to clean here, and until you're clean, I can't tell how bad off you are."

"I'll go to the oasis and wash," I offer.

"Not alone, you won't," she says, straightening before me defiant.

"Okay," I say. "I'm sure that some of the other males will join me."

"Is that what you want?" she asks, biting her lower lip, looking up with half-lidded eyes.

My cock stirs to life as carnal thoughts swell along with it.

"No," I say, voice soft, fingers cupping her cheek.

"Then let's go," she says, glancing around.

I don't have to be asked twice. The rush and glory of victory has my blood singing, and my dragon is ready to claim its sweet reward. My female is ready to give it to me. What else could any male ask for?

She puts her arm around my waist, and together we walk towards the wall.

"Where are you going?" Drosdan calls out.

"Clean up," I say.

"Good idea," he says. "Oasis?"

"Yeah," I reply.

The carnage left behind by the battle litters the landscape as we walk towards the oasis. I'm hyper-aware of the slightest sound or motion, but the trek is thankfully uneventful.

My muscles are sore from everything I asked my body to

do earlier. The Invaders' weapons are designed to stun, much like the ones the Zzlo use, making it clear that part of their intent is to take us alive. If they wanted us dead, we'd have more difficulty fighting them.

The oasis looms ahead. As we walk under its canopy of leaves, the bright night sky dims. The soft sound of water drifts through. We walk quietly, carefully picking each step so as not bring unwanted attention.

Stopping by the edge of the water, I undo my pants one-handed and let them drop. Maeve takes a moment longer to undress, her clothing being both more and infinitely more complicated. My prime cock throbs as I watch her undress.

Could anything be more erotic? As her shirt opens to reveal the cleavage of her breasts an ache forms in my lower belly. Human females are the most exotic of creatures. So strange that their breasts are not protected.

I have dim memory of before, the female Zmaj breasts were not exposed. They were not an object of desire, but strictly for the feeding of young. I don't know why, but the way the human females' breasts jut out, defiant to the world, arouses my desire.

All of the males feel this way about them. Perhaps it is only the novelty of it? The strangeness making it both exotic and erotic?

Her blouse drops over her shoulders and I follow it with my eyes. Appreciating the beautiful line of her neck, down to her shoulder, across her soft arm. A darkness discolors her shoulder where the Invader held her, and rage flames again for a bit, but I push that aside. I have dealt with the fiend who harmed her and will not let him into this moment that belongs to Maeve and me.

Every ounce of her is perfection.

Her body, outlined by the soft silvery light filtering through the leaves, is all I could ever desire.

"Water?" she asks, her eyes cast down, voice oddly demure.

Taking her hand, I lead us into the water. She follows, stepping carefully.

"Oh!" she exclaims, as the water comes up to her waist, and she shivers.

Pulling her closer, I take her first kiss. The sweet taste of her lips is as exotic as she is. The soft fullness of those lips, moist, hints of a fruity flavor on them. My dragon rumbles with desire to devour.

Her arms wrap around my neck, as her legs find their way around my hips.

I walk backwards, carrying her deeper into the water until it's up to my chest. It turns dirty as the filth of battle is washed away.

"I need to wash my hair," Maeve says, breaking our kiss, her lips lingering against mine as if reluctant to leave. "I have Invader goo in it."

"Of course," I murmur.

She unwraps her legs and stands in the water. She leans back dunking her head under the water. When she rises, the water runs across her closed eyes, down her neck, and between the swell of her breasts.

Unable to resist, I lean in and lick along the trail it left behind. Moving across her breasts, I take one of her hard nipples in my mouth and flick it with my tongue.

She groans her pleasure, so I continue giving my full attention to her and it.

Under the water, her hand finds my cock and softly strokes. Returning the favor, I place a hand on the soft, furry mound between her legs, pressing and releasing pressure. I'm rewarded with a new groan and her hips thrusting forward against me.

Continuing in this manner, I'm soft and gentle with her. I don't want to hurt her after the ordeal she's been through.

She moves closer, jumping up and putting her legs around my hips, positioning herself over my cock. Slowly she lowers herself until she is seated and I'm deep within her.

An ultimate paradise. That's how it feels when I enter her. Acutely aware of the bruises and damage to her body I let her set the motion.

The water adds buoyancy to our love making. She pulls herself up and down, impaling herself on me with soft sighs from each of us as she does.

She bites her lower lip, eyes closed. The water moves around us as we make love.

Sensations race through my body that are so much more than our bodies joining. Emotions I didn't know I was capable of feeling intertwine with them creating something new.

"Faster," she pants.

"Are you sure?" I ask, worry coloring my voice.

She opens her eyes, locking them on mine. "Take me," she growls, her eyes alight with delight.

I don't have to be asked twice. Grabbing her hips, I lift her up and slam her down. The water gives a strange resistance to the motion, but that only enhances it.

She kisses me, biting my lower lip and tugging. Her hands scrabble across my scales, scratching as they try to find purchase.

Our lovemaking becomes furious, and I pour everything into it. The fear when I saw her in the hands of that Invader, worry that I was too late, that I would lose her. All my darkest emotions rise up and are cleansed as our bodies join.

"Yes!" she cries out.

I throw my head back and hiss, long and low as my balls explode my pleasure, dumping it all into her. Dancing lights spray out around us that I'm dimly aware of seeing. As the pleasure eases its grip the lights soften but it's then I realize the glass embedded in each of us is sending out rainbow-like sprays of light.

I don't know what it means. Something, I'm sure.

She laughs, shuddering in my arms. I hold her tight until the last vestiges of it passes through both of us.

We hold each other and kiss, soft, gentle kisses until I soften inside of her.

Lifting her up and off she groans. A feeling I share, leaving her is like going out into an empty, lonely world. When I'm with her, in her, I'm complete. When I exit it's as if half of me is left behind inside of her.

It's not physical or logical, but it's the best metaphor I have for how it seems. Strange.

The dim memory of being trapped in a mine pushes up behind it, but I toss that aside. That has no place here, let it stay lost in the fog of the past.

She stands in the water and takes a step back, letting her eyes inspect what she can of me that is above the water line. Tsk'ing she grabs handfuls of sand and scrubs at the dried blood.

We set about the task of caring for each other, cleaning and identifying wounds that will need tending to.

Once we're clean, we walk out of the water and dress. She's limping harder, the bandage on her foot wet now, so I swoop her up into my arms and carry her back to the caves.

The following days pass in a blur. The wall was damaged in the attack, creating even more work to be done.

Errol returns with ideas about how to fix the machine. He

walks up to me a couple of days after his return holding a scrap of paper.

"What?" I say, looking up from the new lochaber I'm forging.

"Can you look at this?" he asks, holding out the scrap of paper.

I take it and look it over.

"Yes?" I ask.

"Can you make it?" he asks.

"Of course," I respond. "I can forge anything."

"Good," he says. "I think it will help stabilize the generator."

"Okay," I say, and he wanders off to his own work.

As I watch him leave, I notice Maeve is working in the garden. An overwhelming urge to be near her hits me, and I run, not questioning it. She's gravity, pulling me towards her. I can't deny or escape it.

She's bent over pulling up some root vegetables when I run up. I grab her by her waist, lift her, and toss her around, turning her midair and catching her. When I pull her close our lips meet, and the sparks fly between us. She returns my kiss with every bit of passion I have for her. Her arms embrace my neck and squeeze.

"What was that?" she asks, laughing as we break the kiss.

"Nothing," I say. "And everything."

"You're impossible," she says, shaking her head.

I put her back on her feet and go back to my work, letting her do the same.

"Wow," I hear Penelope say to her. "He's really into you."

"Yeah," she responds. "He is."

Pleasure tingles across my scales, and I nod to myself as I walk. Yes, yes, I am.

My dragon rumbles contentedly.

Drosdan steps in as I enter my workspace, his arms

crossed over his chest. He clears his throat as he looks over the works in progress.

"Yes?" I ask.

"You and Maeve need to go to the City," he says.

"Why?" I ask, looking at the piles of work I need to do.

"Addison wants you both," he shrugs. "Visidion and Rosalind sent the message, so apparently they're on board with it."

"I'm busy," I counter.

"Right," he says, implacable. "You're the only one that does anything, right?"

Glaring at the insult in his words, I frown, tightening my grip on the hammer lying on my anvil.

"I did not say such a thing," I say.

I am myself, I recount in my head, trying to contain the bijass.

Drosdan is struggling too. The edges of his scales have a reddish hue and he's dropped his hands to his sides where they clench and unclench.

"Right," he says at last. "Well, go."

"Fine," I say.

Together we are stronger, I continue repeating the Edicts, the bijass roaring to respond to the challenge.

Slowly it eases as I focus my thoughts with the Edicts, until at last the bijass retreats, and I remain in control. Sighing, I prepare my forge to be left alone for a few days. I head towards the main cave, expecting to find Maeve working there.

The City is improving. The work being done is starting to show results. Where there was destruction and debris littering the streets, it's being cleared. Water runs in the fountain before the main building, albeit not as it once did.

Do I recall that?

Dimly, I think I do. I can't see it in my mind's eye, but the idea is there when I look at it. That once water spouted high into the air from the statue, showering down into the base. A sign of the prosperity Tajss knew at that time.

It's dim, and the idea of wasting water in such a way makes my scales itch. We were arrogant. Perhaps that's why we had to fall.

"What does she want?" Maeve asks again.

The same question has plagued our entire journey to the City. I don't have answers to it, and neither does she. She's grousing and I know it, but it makes me want to fix it for her.

"I'll handle it," I offer. "I'm sure it's nothing."

"How are you going to handle it?" she snaps.

"I will tell her we are busy and must return to our work at the Caves," I answer.

"Like that's going to help," she says, rolling her eyes.

"I don't understand," I say.

"Visidion and Rosalind want this, you going to stand against them?"

The vehemence in her words makes me stop to consider what she's saying. There is more in the words than I took them for, and I know that I'm not understanding.

"What is upsetting you?" I ask, probing, wanting to understand.

"I don't want to be poked and prodded," she says, exasperation in her voice.

"Then I will not allow it," I say, smiling with joy at having a course of action that will please my female.

"We don't have a choice!" she exclaims, throwing her arms in the air.

"Of course we do," I say. "I will say no, that will be it."

"Gah! You're...." she shakes her head trailing off.

We walk along in an uncomfortable silence as I turn over her words in my head. I don't understand what I missed but it's obvious there is something more than what she is saying.

Her heartbeat thrums in the back of my thoughts, and my scales crawl with sensations of her irritation. It's not me. What is it? Something she's not saying, more to the words? Something she doesn't want to say?

"Maeve?" I ask, giving up on figuring it out.

"What!" she says, her voice sharp.

"What is wrong?" I ask, stopping and facing her full on.

The square around the fountain is empty, and I take advantage of this to confront what is bothering her head on.

She glares at me, arms crossed over her chest, anger playing on her face.

"Gah!" she exclaims, dropping her arms to her side.

Moisture wells in the corners of her eyes, and she looks away. I wait, patient, feeling her emotions as if they are a harsh wind blowing across me.

Patience.

What a strange thing, it's almost enough to distract me from my worry for her. It's not something I've exercised or felt in my memory. A willingness to wait that is different, foreign to me. I know it's but one of the many ways she has changed me.

"I don't want to talk to Addison," she says at last, her lower lip trembling.

"Why?" I ask, placing a hand on her arm in what I hope is a reassuring gesture.

"Do you feel it too?" she asks, her eyes locking onto mine, boring into me.

"Feel it?" I ask, knowing full well what she is asking me but at the same time I want to make sure.

"Yes," she insists, not elaborating.

"I do," I admit. "Always."

"It's not natural," she says, looking away. "It's the glass, it has to be."

"Perhaps," I say. "Or we are merely meant to be together."

"How can that be?" she asks, her eyes seeking mine again. "I'm not a fairy tale princess. I'm just... me. I'm not 'fated' for you. Even if I was, how do we have the unbelievable odds of being right there when the shower happened, and then having the glass embed into us..."

"Because it is what is supposed to be," I say.

"I call bull," she says.

"What is... bull?" I ask, confused.

Maeve's eyes widen, she shakes her head, mouth open then she laughs.

"Good grief, see!" she exclaims. "I traveled trillions of miles from where I should have been born, the unique fortune of being attacked by crazy-ass space pirates, crash-landing on a devastated, hellhole of a planet, and if those odds aren't enough to buck, now you want me to believe that I happen to meet you, happen to get this meteorite glass melded to me, it's too much!"

"Then what would you call it?" I ask, genuinely curious.

"Luck?" she asks, shaking her head again but the doubt in her voice is clear.

"Okay," I agree.

"Okay? That's your answer?"

"Yes, because whether it is fate or luck doesn't matter. If it's luck, then I am the luckiest male in the entirety of all the universe. If it is fate, then still, I am the luckiest male in the entire universe."

"You're impossible," she says, her voice a whisper as she places a hand on my chest.

Warmth radiates out from her touch, and my hearts accelerate in response.

"Perhaps, but did you not just point out how impossible the odds of this are?"

She shakes her head, smiling.

"It's insane," she counters.

"Then we are insane together," I say, tracing the line of her jaw with my finger.

Her plush lips quiver, so I lean down and kiss them, gently, slowly tasting her sweet flavor. She returns the kiss before pulling back.

"Okay," she sighs, shaking her head. "Let's get this over with."

We join hands before we walk into the main building and climb up the broken stairway to Addison, who is waiting for us outside her workspace.

"Oh good, you're here!" she says, smiling broadly.

She ushers us both to follow her. It leads down a short hallway. Glancing in an open door I see two of the Invader bodies lying there stripped of their armor.

Curious, I step inside and look. Their bodies are covered with scars that make symbols. It looks like they've been branded, had those signs burned into their indigo skin. Something about those symbols seems familiar, but I can't place it.

They're muscled, strong-looking, worthy foes. My dragon hums in delight knowing that I've defeated many of them. Squaring my shoulders, I walk over to one and stare down at it, feeling imperious.

"I'm studying those," Addison says. "Those symbols look like things I've found in scraps of information from before the Devastation. I haven't put it all together yet, but one thing is for sure, they've been here before. "

"Yes," I agree, knowing it with certainty, no matter I can't recall how or why.

Shaking my head, I follow Addison out of the room and into an examination room.

"I want to see you two specifically. How have you both been? Any side effects from the glass embedded in you?"

Turning away from the Invader body to look at Maeve, I see her purse her lips and look at the floor.

"Nothing particular," I offer.

Addison looks between the two of us.

"Okay," she says.

The word hangs in the air between the three of us, inviting more detail. I would say more, but it's obvious that Maeve isn't wanting to, so I wait for her lead. I don't want to say what she doesn't want said.

When neither Maeve nor I say more, Addison nods and takes Maeve's arm gently.

"Would you climb up on the table please?" she asks.

Maeve nods and gets onto the examination table. I stand to one side, crossing my arms and watch.

Addison lifts Maeve's shirt enough to reveal the glass in her side. She inspects it closely, passes some strange instruments over it, to what effect I don't know, and at last she lowers Maeve's shirt and nods.

"Okay," she says. "Padraig?"

I take my place on the table and let her do the same to me. I watch Maeve while Addison works. She looks pensive, shifting from foot to foot, eyes darting around the room.

"Something happened," she blurts out and Addison stops her examination of me to listen.

"Yeah?" she encourages Maeve.

"There was an attack, you know," she nods towards the Invader bodies lying behind us.

"Right," Addison nods.

"Well, one of them caught me," she says. "He had me by the arm, held me off the ground, shaking me."

She shivers, her eyes glazing over with the memory. She takes a deep breath and lets it out slowly.

"Anyway," she continues. "He was going to do... whatever with me, but I got mad. I decided to fight back, and when I did the glass... I don't know. There was a bright red flash of light. It pulled the thing's attention, and I think it recognized something."

"Oh," Addison says. "What happened next?"

"Padraig killed it," she says, shaking her head. "It was a moment only but, yeah, it was strange."

Addison nods as she grabs a book from a nearby counter and scribbles furiously in it. My hearts pound. I hadn't noticed the reaction of the glass. Deep in the bijass my only concern was saving Maeve. Frowning deeply, Addison stares at the notebook before she shakes her head.

"Strange," she mutters. "I need more information."

"What do you think it is?" Maeve asks.

She's not telling Addison about the connection or what happens when we're together. I'm not sure why, but I decide I will not speak of it either. Addison walks over to a bench and picks up a small machine.

"I don't know," she says. "We know the glass has electro-magnetic properties. That much is clear. That's why Errol can use it to power the ship force-field generator that is serving as a dome for the Caves. What you're describing though...."

Silence fills the room. A void with nothing more to be said.

"Have you learned anything from studying the body?" I ask, wanting to steer the conversation to something that matters.

"Yeah," she says. "Some."

"What?" Maeve asks, following my lead, she looks gratefully over Addison's head.

"The scars and symbols on their bodies indicate a primal culture. Researching anything from before the Devastation is an exercise in frustration. The information is sparse and apparently Zmaj rarely wrote anything down. It's all stored in the computers that don't work right."

She's leaning close to Maeve, moving the machine in her hand over the glass, probing at the skin around it. Maeve gasps as Addison presses in, and I hiss, instinctively rising to stop Addison.

"It's fine," Maeve mouths, reassuring me.

Forcing my hands to unclench, I resume my position on the table. Addison continues her probing blissfully unaware.

"What I've gathered though… it looks like they've also been thrown back into a more primal state than what they were. When I combine that in with what Rosalind and Visidion have told me about their adventure with the Zzlo and their trip off planet… it's starting to paint a picture."

"Paint a picture?" I ask, unfamiliar with the words put together like that.

"Yeah, you know, tell a story, give me a clue," Maeve says.

"Oh," I say, frowning as I try to make sense of it. The humans use such strange phrasings.

"What do you mean?" Maeve asks.

"The Devastation affected a lot more than Tajss," Addison says. "I believe Tajss was only a piece in a much bigger war that left this entire galaxy devastated."

The fog of the past surges, and something tries to emerge, some lost memory, but it doesn't come through. It leaves a sense of knowing something but not knowing it at the same time.

"What do we do now?" Maeve asks.

"I don't know," Addison says, straightening and shaking

her head. "Rosalind and Visidion are working on plans but... we need to know more."

"The Invader said they want everything," Maeve says.

Addison goes to the notebook and writes that down.

"Anything else?" she asks.

Maeve shakes her head negative with her eyes locked on me. The connection between us throbs.

"If anything happens, I need you both to let me know," Addison says. "Anything. Please."

She stresses the last two words, and it makes me wonder if she knows that there is more going on with us than we're saying, but she doesn't press the issue further.

11

MAEVE

*T*he land rover bumps across some rocks as we travel back to the Caves. We haven't said much since leaving the City, both of us deep in our own thoughts.

Strange how comfortable a silence can be between two people. If it's natural, there's no need to fill the void.

If Tajss wasn't the only planet affected by the Devastation, what does that mean?

We know the Zzlo were raiding the planet, but they've not been seen in a while. Now there are new Invaders, apparently. I don't know much at all about what happened with Rosalind and Visidion. Only rumors and innuendo—what Addison said was more than I'd heard before.

They were taken off planet? Where? How did they get back?

So many questions, and no answers for any of them.

"Why do we not tell Addison about us?" Padraig asks, breaking the long silence.

"I'm not sure," I admit, blunt honesty. "It seems so... personal."

He nods but doesn't say anything else for quite a while.

The terrain outside the transport passes along, unchanging for the most part. Sand and more sand, the only variation is the ever-shifting striations of color, drifting with the blowing of the winds.

"If she needs to know?" he asks. "If it would help?"

"Do you think it will?" I counter.

His brow furrows. "I do not know," he says.

"Nor do I," I admit. "I want to understand it better myself."

I don't say the other part of that thought. I want to know if the glass is why I'm falling for him. Is it influencing me mentally as well as whatever is happening physically?

He's changing. Having an outside perspective, I see it clearly. Am I? Are we being drawn together by the strange, outside force of this meteorite glass?

How do I know?

I want to believe that we belong together. That what I feel for him is real, natural. I think it is, but then there is doubt. We don't know what this glass is doing to us.

Suddenly I'm thrown against the restraining harness as Padraig brakes the transport. It skids on loose sand before coming to a halt.

"Are you okay?" he asks.

"Yes, what was that?"

He's looking out the window, so I follow his gaze. Ahead of us a pack of sismis swarms around a massive carcass. The lights of the transport have driven them into the air where they swoop back and forth.

"That is a lot of meat," he says. "If I can drive the sismis off, we can harvest it for the Tribe."

"Good plan," I agree.

He rummages in the back and finds a torch. He takes a few steps away from the transport, and then he belches a bit of fire to light it. Watching him do this creates a weird sensation in me. It's so foreign and strange. Out of the blue, I wonder what would happen if he ever did that while we were kissing?

Ugh, stop it Maeve, I admonish myself.

Padraig twists the torch in his hand until it's flaming brightly, and then he smiles.

"Wait here," he says, a devilish light in his eyes and a childish grin on his face.

"What are you—"

He runs before I can finish the question, brandishing the torch and whooping like a madman. He races into the pack of sismis, some of whom are feasting and some circling in the air, waving the torch wildly.

The sismis screech, hitting a note that makes my skin crawl, as they take to the air and circle chaotically, all but running into each other. One of them takes off, then the rest of the pack follows the apparent leader.

Padraig turns to me, grinning from ear to ear.

"Did you know that was going to work?" I ask.

"Nope," he replies without a hint of abashment at his brash actions.

"Wow," I say, shaking my head before climbing into the transport and getting tools to harvest the meat.

We work for what feels like hours. The moon is dropping low by the time we've finished the harvest. There's enough meat here, once smoked, to feed the Tribe for most of a month, at least. It's a fortunate find. Meat is getting harder to come by, forcing the hunters to wander farther afield.

Covered in goo mixed with sweat, I settle back into my seat. Padraig starts the transport, and we're on our way again. It's not long at all before my eyes drift shut.

"Addison said that about the entire galaxy?" Delilah asks, picking apart the details of my story.

Sighing, I wipe my brow free of sweat, not that it will last. The smoldering smoker has driven the heat inside the cavern to almost unbearable levels.

"Yeah," I say.

"That sounds horrifying," Penelope observes.

"You saw one of them up close," Delilah says. "What was it like?"

"Scary," I say, honestly. "Its eyes were, I don't know, feral yet intelligent? Cruel. Can eyes be cruel?"

"I'd say so," Penelope says, opening the door to the smoker and using the makeshift tongs to pull out the meat that is done in that one.

"Definitely," Delilah says, nodding but I don't miss the quiver in her voice. That's when I remember, she was abducted by the Zzlo.

"Are you okay?" I ask, placing a hand on her arm.

"Sure," she says, too quick, not meeting my eyes.

"Why wouldn't she be?" Kate ask, coming back from carrying finished meat to storage.

"Nothing," I say, not wanting to tell Delilah's story for her.

Kate stares, pursing her lips, eyes moving to each of us.

"We're talking about the alien Miss Ballsy here almost got taken by," Delilah says. "It's scary no matter what kind of brave face she tries to put on it."

"Oh, right," Kate says. "How are you? Did it hurt you?"

"Bruised, mostly," I say, waving it off. "I won't deny it was scary. That thing…"

I don't have to fake the shiver that runs down my spine. I've seen those bottomless eyes every night in my nightmares.

"We'll be fine," Delilah says firmly.

"Right," Penelope says.

The four of us stand in a tight circle, reassuring each other silently until Delilah grabs me and pulls me into a hug.

"Don't be a fool anymore, okay?" she asks, squeezing me so tight I can't take a breath.

Kate and Penelope join the hug, making it heart-warming and awkward at the same time.

"We *are* going to be fine," Kate says.

"The Dragons won't let anything happen to us," Penelope says with total certainty.

"Thanks gals," I wheeze.

The group hug breaks up, and we resume our duties of preparing the meat for storing. The mood is lighter now, which is reflected in the conversation. Inevitably, it seems, it breaks down into a debate about whether the Stars Wars movies are better than the Star Trek universe.

"I like the comic book movies," Kate throws in, and we all groan.

"Sure, but that's not sci-fi," Delilah argues. "Adding those in would break the fundamental base of the argument."

The rest of the day passes without any resolution being reached to any of the questions raised. I don't think there is any way to resolve them, but they make a fun way to pass the time. Personally, I like all of them, they're each unique and bring their own enjoyment.

Mostly, I miss the vids from the ship. I know a lot of them have been salvaged, but I don't think anyone has gotten a player working so that they can be watched, so they're pointless.

When we sit down to dinner, the work of the day has everyone feeling tired but cheerful. Olivia sits at one end of the table with Zoe on her lap, feeding the growing girl. She's getting bigger all the time with a cute factor that grows exponentially, as she does.

The camaraderie of mealtime is a treat. I look forward to

it at the end of each day. Simple, yes, but it's so different than life on the ship. Even the girls assigned to the same dorm as I was didn't do our meals together.

It would have been hard because we all had different jobs and worked various shifts, but not even at the end of the week did our schedules match up. Sometimes on holidays we'd do a dinner, but it never felt like this. This is special. It brings us all together as a community and provides a welcome respite from the stress of surviving here on Tajss.

As the meal wraps up, some of the men pull out drums that they've made and begin playing a song. Most of the Zmaj hum along, adding a chorus of sound. I've heard the music before, but don't know if there are words to it or not. They never voice any, using their voices, the rustles of their wings, and shifting of their tails on the sand to add layers.

It's exotic, interesting, and always gets us girls tapping our toes. Delilah and I are clapping along, keeping time, and I'm paying attention to her to help me stay on the beat, because I suck at that, when a shadow blocks out the candlelight.

Padraig stands in front of me holding his hand out, bowing at his waist. Looking up at him, wide-eyed, my cheeks burn red hot, and I can't get a breath in. He can't be asking me to dance. He can't, because I can't.

Desperate, I look at Delilah, who is zero help. She laughs and pushes on my arm.

"Maeve, Maeve, Maeve," Kate starts the chant but is quickly joined by the other girls.

"Guys," I protest.

Padraig doesn't wait. Taking my hand, he whisks me onto my feet and pulls me out in front of the drummers.

I haven't seen the Zmaj dance before making it even more awkward.

He's surprisingly light on his feet considering his massive

size. Roughly he pulls me close, one hand on the small of my back forcing me against his body. The difference in our heights means my breasts are pressed against his lower stomach. He squeezes, holding me in place, then lifts so my feet are barely touching the ground.

His wings spread out, his tail lifts behind him, and he spins me around smoothly, then slides to the side. It's a heady experience, and in moments I'm lost in the beats of it.

Our eyes lock onto each other as we glide in time with the throbbing beats of the drums. The voices of the Zmaj weaving in and out of the rhythm are hypnotic. In moments, my embarrassment is forgotten.

His large cock is stiff, digging into me, but even that only adds to the experience. A sure sign of not only his desire, but when coupled with the fire in his eyes, his passion for me.

The sound of the drums changes, becoming faster, and he looks to the right, pulling my arm out straight. Moving along with him, I turn my head to face in the same direction. He leaps, carrying me along, and his wings cause us to drift through the air impossibly far. We land lightly, spinning, and he lowers into a crouch as he does, taking me down with him.

As the spin stops, he is rising again and leaps back in the other direction. The drums beat harder, faster, and the voices raise in pitch. He repeats the move, but on the next leap, he spins us in the air. I yelp, not expecting the move, as my stomach feels like it's left somewhere behind us.

We land, lightly as ever, and he sways back and forth, holding me close. His eyes bore into mine, desire burning in them, yes, but there is something more, deep inside them. A fire that isn't desire alone.

A shiver runs through my limbs, and the hair on my arms stands on end. Warmth forms in my core and burns its way out. My fingers find the strong line of his jaw and trail along it as we move.

The rough edges of his scales are a fascinating texture, and I want to touch him everywhere. The watching crowds are forgotten. There is only the two of us, dancing in the stars.

The music stops with a sudden finality, and Padraig ends the dance by setting me gently on the ground. He takes a step back and gives a partial bow, his eyes never leaving mine.

Cheeks burning hot, I smile, unsure what the proper response is to his formality. Awkwardly, I return the half-bow to him. He smiles, takes my hand, and as one we turn towards the caves.

Only then do I realize all eyes are on us. The smiles on the girls faces and the delight in their eyes fills me with an all new rush of wanting to hide. The couples are each one hugging each other—Kate and Errol are particularly close. She catches my eyes and nods encouragingly.

The audience bursts into applause and cheers.

"Go Maeve!" Delilah shouts excitedly.

Zoe stumbles out of the assembled crowd, toddling her way to the open space between the audience and where we stand. She holds her hands out to either side, her small wings extending, and she twirls with an almost grace that is so adorable I'm about to burst.

Oohs and ahhs greet her attempt to mimic the dance until she tries to leap like Padraig did, but she doesn't quite make it. She falls to the ground hard, skidding across the packed sand. She sits up, looking around, unsure if she should cry or try again.

"You got this, Zoe!" Kate encourages her.

Zoe smiles, gurgles something unintelligible, then rises to her feet unsteadily. She pirouettes then falls on her butt. Olivia steps forward then, scooping her up.

"You're a beautiful dancer!" Olivia says, kissing the top of her head.

"Momma," she says, grinning.

"Yes, baby love," Olivia says. "Now it's time for bed, okay?"

"Momma," Zoe says.

Olivia heads for her room, and the assembled Tribe members follow the cue. We all have duties tomorrow, and sleep is good.

Hand in hand, Padraig and I go to his room with a tacit agreement.

As the door closes behind us, I go over to his bed and pause. As I look around the sparsely furnished room, something inside me shifts.

I'm happy.

No matter how much lip service I've always paid to making Tajss my home, knowing that we're stuck here one way or the other, there was always a level of making the best of the bad to it.

Now… it's not making the best of the bad. It's making my life.

Padraig comes up behind and wraps his arms around me, encircling me. He nuzzles at my neck kissing up to my ear and nibbling on the lobe. I lean my head to one side, giving him full access.

His hands roam freely, and I welcome them as he explores my body over my clothes. One hand presses against the mound between my legs, putting a delicious pressure on my clit.

"Are you mine?" he whispers in my ear.

Everything stops, my breath, my heart, time freezes.

"Yes," I say, a flush racing up my neck as suddenly I feel shy. "I can't deny it, Padraig, I am yours."

"And I am yours," he responds, sweeping me off my feet and lying me on the bed.

We make love and then lie in the afterglow, basking in each other's warmth. I'm drifting to sleep when a loud pop sounds.

"What!" I cry out, sitting straight up in bed, adrenalin pushing away sleep.

My heart pounds, and in the back of my head I feel his hearts matching the rhythm of mine.

"Wait here," he says, slipping his pants on, and then he glances over his shoulder. "Please."

"I wouldn't have it any other way," I smile, appreciating the change.

12

PADRAIG

$\mathcal{M}$y hearts pound as soon as I step through the door. The whine of ships overhead fills the night air. One glance is all it takes. The shield is down, again. The Invaders' ships are coming, and we are defenseless.

"Maeve, go to the main cave! Get the others!" I yell over my shoulder.

I don't bother taking the ramp down. I leap off the edge, spread my wings, and catch the wind, gliding down, pulling my lochaber as I do.

I land next to Ragnar and we exchange a dark look. Melchior and Bashir run up to us.

"Tajss isn't happy with this," Bashir says. "They want its secrets."

Melchior grimaces as Bashir asserts this. Ragnar and I exchange a questioning look but neither of us say anything about it.

"Who can try to fix the shield?" Ragnar barks.

"Assemble!" Drosdan's voice booms through the night.

"I can," Samil's voice comes out of nowhere.

As one, we all look at the smaller Zmaj, doubt clear on

our faces. I have to give him credit when he doesn't flinch under our gaze.

"I've watched Errol," he says. "I can do this!"

He doesn't wait for permission, turning and running. I watch for a moment and realize that he's changing. Or I am. There's no time to think about it.

"If he doesn't get it working…" Melchior trails off, there's no need to say more.

"They're landing outside the wall," Drosdan says, cutting off the thought.

My hearts leap, and I look at the cliff wall. Maeve is holding Penelope's hand as they race to the main cave.

Be safe my love, I will protect you.

"Padraig, guard the cave," Ragnar says. "Protect them."

His words carry a sacred charge in them. Our females are there. He holds out his arm, and I clasp it, wrist to wrist. The rest of the Zmaj race off to the wall, and I move into the cave. Stepping into the shadow I take up a position right inside, using the dark to hide my presence, hoping to take any enemy by surprise.

The sounds of battle engage past the wall. I stare so hard it should burn its way through the wall, but it doesn't.

A whistling sound reaches my ears over the din of battle. I've never heard anything like it before. Tilting my head to the side I close my eyes and focus on identifying it. It's close. Too close.

Three Invaders drop out of the sky from ropes and land a few feet from the cave entrance. One of them holds up a closed fist, then jerks it down. The other two with him take up stances behind him and as a unit they approach the cave, cautiously.

The thrill rises as the bijass surges in my thoughts. They think to take us unawares. They want my treasure. The surprise they are in for brings a smile to my face. Deep in the cave, the hushed whispers of the females drift to me. Out of them I hear Maeve's voice, adding fuel to the fire.

Mine. None will touch her.

Gripping my lochaber tighter, I silently wait.

I watch my enemy move, waiting for an opening. They're skilled. A tight unit working as one, but they have no idea what they face. None will best me, not with my female in danger.

The leader's foot crosses into the shadow of the cavern, his gun in front of him sweeping back and forth.

One step, and I grab the gun, twisting it hard and fast. The sound of bone snapping is followed by his cry of pain. He lets go of the weapon, or tries, but I jerk it towards me, pulling him closer.

I slam my left fist into his face, and blood explodes from under his helmet. He drops to the ground.

The two with him fire their weapons, but the shots go wide, unaimed. I leap and land between them. After grabbing their shoulders, I slam them together.

Their helmets mitigate most of the damage, but they're slowed. The one on my right fires and the electrical burst of his weapon hits me in the chest. Blue lightning plays across my scales, numbing nerves.

My arm drops to my side, refusing to respond. The close proximity of the shot magnifies the effects of the weapon. Roaring, I punch with my left, slamming it against the metal of his helmet.

The metal rings like a bell, but my attention is on him, and the other opponent regains his senses, firing at my exposed side. More of the blue lightning hits me in the hip, and my left leg loses feeling. The knee tries to give out, and I remain up by force of will alone.

Swinging my lochaber one-handed, the blade connects

but slides across his armor, not finding purchase. It does drive him back, gaining me room to maneuver.

My opponents step back, trying to aim. I can't give them time. If even a single shot hits my head, this is over.

I clench my right fist, pump it open and closed, forcing blood down the arm, making it come back to life while turning a circle with my lochaber extended to keep them both in view.

A semblance of life returns to my numb arm, it tingles and hurts as it recovers, but there's no time. Grabbing my lochaber two handed I twirl it over my head and down, weaving a defensive pattern that moves up and down, around and around as I continue spinning.

It keeps them at bay and creates confusion, making it harder for them to lock in their shot.

Around and around we go, all of us looking for an opening. One mistake by any of us, and this is over. It's all it will take for either side to end the other.

Feinting at one of the Invaders, I shift and swing low, but he jumps over the blade. The second shoots. The shot goes wide but grazes my wings as it does. They pulse with pain then fall numb and useless.

I can't hold out for long. They'll wear me down eventually by virtue of numbers alone.

The fight has taken us deeper into the cave. I have to end this before they find the females or the crevasse to the epis.

Swinging wildly, I abandon form and style in favor of barbaric rage. Roaring, I charge the closest one to me, bringing the lochaber overhead and swinging it down two-handed, intending to cleave my opponent.

Inside his helmet, his eyes widen, his mouth drops open, he brings the rifle up as he stumbles backwards, and then the sound of electricity fills the air. He screams and drops before I hit him.

"Look out!" Delilah screams, standing behind the Invader wide-eyed with a long stick in her hand, the end of which crackles with arcing electricity.

Shifting in an instant, I instinctively duck, spinning on my heel with lochaber extended and circling with me. It catches the other Invader at the knees, slicing by fortune as much as intent, through a weak point in its armor, dropping it.

I don't hit it before its shot goes off though, and behind me I hear Delilah scream—then silence.

I finish the Invaders swiftly before looking.

Delilah lies in a heap on the ground, not moving. Their weapons are intended to stun, but I don't know how they will react on a human body. I'm certain they've set the power of their weapons for a Zmaj.

My hearts pound as I move towards her, slowly. She has to be okay. I can't have failed her.

Emptiness forms in my core and a strange, creeping sensation follows. Dim memories surge out of the bijass fog, being trapped, left alone, waiting to die.

Crouching next to Delilah's still form, moving my hand towards her, I'm forcing myself to do what I know must be done. I touch her cheek first—she's warm. Hope forms as I move my fingers to her neck. Beneath them, I feel the soft pulse. Relief rushes through me, and I rock back onto my heels, exhaling a breath I didn't realize I'd been holding.

"Is she?" Maeve asks, stepping out of the deep darkness of the cave.

"No," I answer.

She nods, biting her lip. "Good."

Penelope and Inga come up beside her.

"Get her back down there, I can't leave my post here," I say, my eyes landing on the stick she used on the Invader. "What is that?"

" Something Kate's been working on," Inga says. "I guess we can tell her it works."

Nodding, I let it go, for now, after all, it did work. The mix of emotions I feel about having the females put themselves into danger, or participate in battle, fights with the instinct to keep them safe.

Lana and Astarot fight and hunt together. It's strange, but he handles it. Maybe my belief is wrong? Instinct roars against it, but doubt creeps in, making it less.

Pushing aside my considerations on it, I go back to my post, staring out of the cave's shadows, searching for fresh threats. The sounds of battle continue outside the wall.

The ships hover overhead, not bringing their guns to bear. Why? The shield is down. If they use them, there is nothing we can do.

Staring at the hovering ships and the massive guns mounted to them my mind races. There has to be a reason. The guns would end this battle. They would win.

They want something then. Something that the massive guns would harm or destroy.

Epis?

No, the epis is deep in the cave. The guns wouldn't harm it.

There has to be another reason. They're putting themselves at risk. We've killed many of them already.

Us? Are they slavers like the Zzlo?

That doesn't fit what I know either.

The whistling sound comes again, interrupting my thoughts. Another team of three lands inside the wall, dropping from above on their ropes. Anger rages inside me.

I can't find their motives, but I can destroy them. I'm tired of the threat they represent. This has to end now.

This team doesn't come for the cave. They glance towards it, but move off to the workstations along the cliff wall.

If they won't come to me, then I will go to them.

I go running out of the cave, leap into the air, and glide. Silent death coming from above. Lochaber held ready.

One of them glances back and shouts right before I land behind them. They turn in perfect synchronicity and fire as a single unit. All hit their target. Blue lightning plays across my chest, sending numbing waves through my body.

My arms, legs, and wings are heavy and sluggish, refusing to move as they should. My lochaber slips from my fingers, as I'm unable to keep my grasp on it.

They spread out, one moving to cover each side of me, guns aimed, the other approaches cautiously.

"Padraig!" Maeve's scream cuts through the night air and through the din of the battle happening beyond the wall.

The bijass rises and I give myself over to it fully, embracing my primal nature. I drop to my knees and touch the sand of Tajss. The meteorite glass in my chest suddenly lights up, a reddish glow pulsing. Power surges through my muscles, fighting off the sluggishness.

A pair of feet enter the edge of my vision. Panting, I wait a moment longer, letting them come closer.

Roaring I leap up, grabbing the Invader's head. Surprise widens its black eyes, drops its jaw. In a single motion, I snap its neck before it can emit a cry.

It falls with a thud.

Move. Move faster!

My dragon roars triumph and distantly I hear the sound of it coming from my throat as I leap on the next closest one. Grabbing the gun it tries to bring to bear, I jerk down, then pull it towards me, applying such force that the arms holding it break.

It swings its other arms at me, knives appearing, but I punch it in the face.

It stumbles back, blood pouring, eyes wide. Seeing its fear fuels my action.

When I start towards it, I'm hit in the back. Numbness takes my left wing and my left arm drops, no longer obeying my commands.

I whirl around as the one behind me fires again, but my motion causes it to miss. It's all the time I need. I leap up, swing my tail, and hit it alongside its head.

A loud crack and it drops to the ground.

Roaring, I throw my arms wide, welcoming all challengers. None can defeat me! I am!

Three more Invaders drop from the sky on their black ropes. I welcome them with a hiss and a loud cry. More for me to defeat. More to show my treasure who is the dominant one.

They keep a distance, circling me.

"Cowards!" I yell, circling with them.

They move until each of them is by one of the ones I've downed. Guns staying true to me, they kneel and hook ropes to the bodies.

One of them tugs on his rope, and all six of them rise into the sky.

"NO!" I rage.

I leap at one of them and grab its boot before it's out of reach. I'm being pulled up along with it. It screeches, kicking at me with its free foot. Slamming over and over onto my hand.

Pain is distant and doesn't matter. Defeating him is all that matters. He challenged me. Escaping isn't one of his options.

As I rise into the sky, up towards their ship, a sudden thought occurs through the rage.

Their leader is in there. If I defeat him, then I dominate them all.

A smile spreads across my face.

Yes. I will defeat the Invaders single-handedly!

The foot slams into my closed hand again, and something snaps. I lose my grip and I'm falling.

I try to spread my wings, but the left refuses to respond. I'm twirling towards the ground, out of control.

As it races up at me with its promise of pain and possible death, all I can think of is Maeve. Her face drifts across my mind's eye and stays. Her smile, her soft perfect skin.

No, I cannot die.

She needs me, I am her protector. This is not how I end.

Gritting my teeth, I push every ounce of will I have into the numb, unresponsive wing.

It twitches. A moment later it opens. With both wings I can stop my wild spin and drift to the ground, landing in a three-point touchdown.

Silence.

I turn in a circle to look for new threats. My eyes lock on Maeve, running out of the cave.

In the back of my head is the galloping sound of her heart. She skids to a stop in front of me, her hands touching my chest, warm and cool at the same time.

When I look at her through the fog, anger lashes out.

"Get back," I order her. "It's not safe."

"Padraig," she says, her voice soft, as she shakes her head in denial.

"No," I growl, grabbing her by her waist and lifting her off her feet.

I run for the cave, carrying her on my side. I have to get her to safety. If they drop from the sky or they fire their guns....

She struggles, but I don't have time, not while she's in danger.

I set her down inside the cave, grasping her shoulders, my eyes boring into hers.

"Deeper, you must be safe!" I command.

"Don't lose yourself," she says, her voice cracking. "Come back to me." Moisture falls from her eyes, trailing rivulets down her cheeks.

The fog recedes, and I see her clearly for the first time without the red haze. She's scared, worried for me. My chest swells and indescribable sensations race through my body.

"I'm fine," I assure her. "Maeve, please, go deep. Keep the others safe. You be safe."

I plead with her, willing her to understand.

"It's too dangerous," she says. "Don't go."

"I must," I answer her. "I will keep you safe."

"Padraig..." her voice falters. She touches my cheek, her fingers trailing lightly along my jaw. "I can't live without you."

Everything stops. I can't take a breath. My hearts don't beat. A soft blue light glows from my chest, matched by the glass in her side. The connection between us pulses with life, and the truth of her words cuts through the remnants of the bijass.

"Nor I, you," I answer.

She nods, nothing more either of us can say or do. Pursing her lips, she turns and moves deeper into the cave. My gaze lingers on her until I force myself to look away and return to my post.

The transport barrels through the gate moments after I get back there. Full speed, it goes towards the workstations, skidding to a stop, sand spraying.

Kate and Errol leap out of it carrying something between them, racing for the machine and Samil. They all work, and in a few moments, there's a loud clicking sound followed by a hum, and the shield reappears.

The Zmaj cheer as they retreat back inside the wall. The Invaders fire a few shots at the shield, using their massive cannons at last, and then it's over. The ships race away, and we're left alone. For now.

Once I'm certain they're gone, I run deep into the cave to the females.

"Are they gone?" Penelope asks.

"Yes," I announce. "We are safe."

Cheers meet my announcement, echoing off the cave walls. Maeve rushes over and throws her arms around me. When I crush her against my chest, our hearts beat in time with each other. Holding her, nothing else matters.

"I'm not sleeping tonight," Lana says.

"We'll set up patrols," Drosdan announces, returning from the battle outside the wall. "They knew the shield was down."

"But how?" Delilah asks, the question we all have.

All of us look at each other, but no one has an answer.

"A spy?" Maeve asks, looking up at me.

"Perhaps," Ragnar says. "We'll need to patrol out far enough to catch them if they are."

"Concentric rings," Drosdan says. "I want three rings with pairs of two. This isn't war parties, but scouts. Each pair within shouting distance of the next. If anything is spotted, relay it back to the center. We'll take them in force, not engage them alone."

No one argues with his logic.

"I want to help," Maeve says.

Her words pull my attention to her. Instinct roars that she can't be outside the wall. No way I'll let her be put in danger like that.

The resolve on her face makes it clear how anything I say to that effect will be received.

"Me too," Delilah says.

All of the males look at each other, and I read the same

thought on their faces. None of us want to put the females into obvious danger.

"It's not safer here," Melchior offers, holding his hands out and motioning around. "The Invaders are obviously targeting the cave."

A round of nods meets his statement. I can't offer any argument against his logic. It's true that they keep coming at it.

"We have the stun sticks," Maeve says, pulling one of them up and holding it before her. Electricity crackles across two metal points on the end of it. "We're not defenseless."

"And there's not enough of you guys to pair up, patrol, and have watchers inside the wall," Penelope says.

"They're right," Drosdan says begrudgingly.

Silence sits heavily among us as each of us struggles to come to terms with the reality of the situation.

Maeve's eyes bore into me with a fiery intention that warms my scales. Her bravery is admirable, and I can't help but acknowledge it. She is everything a male could want. Fierce, protective, and willing to do whatever must be done for the survival of the group.

Survival of the group matters. The Second Edict. She embodies it to a degree I still strive to achieve.

"Right," I say. "Maeve is with me."

No one argues with my statement, and Drosdan nods his agreement. The other males pair up with a female and we walk towards the wall.

"We'll take the furthest circle," I offer as we pass through the gate.

Maeve and I walk into the open desert as I count out paces in my head. We walk in a heavy silence until Penelope and Bashir are a blot in the darkness. Nodding to myself as much as for Maeve, I change directions and start a patrol on an arc that will cover our range.

"Thank you," Maeve says, breaking the silence.

"Huh?" I ask.

"Thank you," she repeats, placing a hand on my arm.

The warmth of her touch on my scales is electric arousing instant desire.

"For?" I ask.

"Not arguing. I know you wanted to," she says, chuckling.

"Okay," I say.

"I get it," she says. "It's instinct isn't it?"

"A male protects his female," I answer.

"Right," she says, nodding. "Pretty much what I thought."

"Is that wrong?" I ask.

"No," she says, a thoughtful note to her words. I wait for her to continue. "It's not wrong, but it has its place. I'm not fragile. None of us are. We're survivors. You have to see that, accept that.

I don't know what it was like.... before, but this is a new world, for you and for us too."

"So it is," I agree.

The fog of memory and time throbs, pregnant with things I don't want to recall. Female Zmaj are so distant in my memory now as to be almost a myth.

We walk in silence until we've gone as far as I plan, then turn and start back in the other direction, scanning the area as we walk.

"There's something else too," she says at last.

"Oh?" I ask.

"Do you feel it?" she asks.

She doesn't have to specify, I know what she means. The connection between us is the only thing she can mean. That pulsing thread, the sound of her heart that's always there, behind my thoughts, beating with my own hearts.

"Yes," I say, acknowledging it once more.

She exhales heavily, as if she'd been holding her breath while waiting for me to respond.

"Good," she says, nodding and biting her lip. "I was worried I was going crazy."

"You are not, my love," I say, pausing our patrol and turning to look at her fully for the first time. "Never."

She smiles, her eyes shiny in the soft light of the stars. The silvery light casts highlights in her hair, makes her skin look so soft, it makes my hearts ache with desire and more, love that has no boundaries.

"It's growing," she says, putting hand lightly on my chest. "Changing. I felt... I had to be out here with you. I don't know why, it's not logical. It's a feeling but more, a calling? Maybe?"

She shakes her head and looks down.

"You are not crazy," I say.

"You all think Bashir is," she counters.

That gives me pause. It's true. We don't say it out loud, but most of the Zmaj have tacitly decided that Bashir has something wrong with him. His belief that the planet is alive, and that we are extensions of it or whatever it is he thinks.

Is this what he feels though?

A connection with... something the same as I feel for Maeve? That would change my thoughts on it, but how can I be sure?

"It's not that we think he's crazy," I say.

"Then what is it?"

"We don't understand it," I give the most honest answer I can.

"Yeah," she agrees. "I don't either but this... command... is coming from somewhere. I can't say where or why or even how but it's... real. Definitely real. If this is then maybe Bashir is, I don't know, onto something?"

"Perhaps," I say, unwilling to fully commit to the idea.

"Yeah," she says, dropping her hand from my chest as she

turns away. "Or I'm crazy and he's crazy and we're off to the loony bin."

"No," I say, grabbing her by her shoulders and turning her to me more forcefully than I intended. "No."

I shake my head, staring into her eyes, willing her to understand. Her lip trembles, and moisture forms in the corners of her eyes.

I don't know what to do, so I do the only thing I can to make her understand.

I kiss her.

I kiss her with all my passion, all my desire, but more than all of that, I kiss her with all the love in my hearts. So much love, if I don't get it out of my body I'm going to explode.

I kiss her soft, willing lips, pushing my certainty into her.

Kissing away her doubts.

Kissing away her fears.

I kiss her with all that I am, and all that I know we can be.

She responds in kind, her arms wrapping around my neck as she rises onto her toes, giving herself over to me fully.

Suddenly she stiffens and breaks the kiss.

"There," she whispers, pointing, fear lacing the single word.

Following the direction she indicates, I shift my eye lenses to bring in clarity of vision, and something shifts on the sand. It's barely a motion, but I know it's there.

I bend my knees, pull my lochaber, take one step and leap, wings spreading to catch air. It carries me silently towards my target.

Right before I land, the sand explodes, and an Invader leaps up to meet my attack.

It doesn't bother with its guns, opting to meet me in hand-to-hand combat. It's six arms flail as it flies up. We crash into each other in midair, tumbling head over heels, fighting for the upper hand.

It twists and turns, wriggling its way onto the top. I slam into the ground with its gnashing teeth snapping over my face, trying to find purchase.

Scrabbling to find a hold along its smooth armor, I get a grip on its neck. It punches me along my sides and in my stomach. My scales mitigate the damage, but the blows are adding up. A rib breaks, and then it brings a knee up into my crotch.

Thought explodes into blinding white pain and the bijass races forward, instinctively taking over.

Roaring I stop trying to find purchase and move it off me. Instead I grab it and pull it tight against my chest, squeezing it with every ounce of strength I have.

"Padraig!" Maeve's cry cuts through to me, but I can't turn to her—the enemy must be destroyed.

I'm stronger. It must succumb to me.

A crackling sound is followed by a snap, and the monster goes limp in my arms.

I push it off of me and climb to my feet.

Maeve stands with her stun stick held before her watching the creature, then looking at me wide-eyed.

"Are you hurt?" I ask, closing with her.

"No," she says, breathing heavily. "Are you okay?"

"Yeah," I say, as a sharp pain stabs through and my voice cracks.

"You're hurt!" she cries, running her hands over me.

"It's nothing," I respond, wincing when her hand passes over the broken rib.

"It's not nothing," she says, turning back towards the cliff.

She yells for Bashir. He and Penelope come running out of the darkness in moments.

"Couldn't wait, huh?" Bashir asks, looking at the Invader.

"He was very impatient," I answer.

Bashir kneels next to the body, placing a hand on it.

"Tajss is pleased," he announces, then hoists the body over his shoulder.

I stare at Bashir as he walks away. His casual pronouncement rings with a strange truth in my ears. I take Maeve's hand, and together we walk back home.

13

MAEVE

"What do you think?" Penelope asks, standing to one side and pointing at her creation.

"Uhm," I say, trying to come up with something nice to say.

I can see the intention behind the thing, and maybe in some kind of abstract way it accomplishes that goal, but to me it's ugly. Really ugly.

"It's not bad," Delilah says, pursing her lips and giving me the slightest shake of her head.

"Right," I agree, biting off any other thoughts.

"I know," Penelope says, deflating. "This is harder than I thought it'd be."

"Maybe Tajss hates Christmas," Kate offers. "So we have to out-create it. To that end, I think it's beautiful."

Penelope brightens at her words.

"Maybe if I add another pole to the center, then I could attach some of those twigs we gather at the oasis. Oh, and the leaves of that one plant growing in the garden, they're almost like pine sticks. Maybe they would help flesh it out?"

Her voice grows with excitement as she goes on. The

three of us nod along with her. I don't know about the other two, but it sounds to me like she's creating the Frankenstein's monster of Christmas as a tree.

Does it matter though? Is Christmas about the tree and the things, or is it really about the idea?

"I think that sounds great," I say, changing my own position on the tree.

It may look more like an abstract skeleton of a tree blasted by the engines of a jet fighter but that doesn't matter. The heart and love she's putting into it does.

"What is that?" Padraig's deep voice asks, rumbling across my skin and making my heart pound.

Tingles race across my skin. His presence is a warmth that embraces me, and I welcome it.

"A Christmas tree," Kate says.

"Almost one," Penelope adds.

"Oh," he says, tilting his head to one side and narrowing his eyes.

"What's up?" I ask, changing the subject before he can say something hurtful, even if I'm sure it would be unintentional.

"Drosdan wants some of us to go talk to Visidion and Rosalind," he says, looking away from the makeshift tree.

"Oh," I say, an empty feeling in my stomach.

"I'd like you to come," he adds, as if sensing my regret.

"Oh," I say, but this time with enthusiasm. "Sure."

"Kate, they want you too," he adds. "Bashir and Errol are coming along, and they want us to bring the new weapons."

"Sure," Kate agrees easily.

"I'll keep working on in it," Penelope says.

"Sounds great," Delilah says. "I'll see if I can come up with any ideas too."

Padraig holds his hand out, and I take it, walking out of the cave with him.

"Are we walking?" I ask.

"No, we'll take the transport," he says. "We need to get there and get back."

"Good," I agree.

There's a lot to do. There's always a lot to do. Days on Tajss fly by because there's no time to contemplate. Survival is first and foremost, and that takes a lot of work and effort to accomplish. Gardening, hunting, preparing meals, making the daily things we need, it all takes time.

None of that takes into consideration the problems with the strange Invaders either.

When I climb into the transport, we all nod to each other, then ride in an uneasy silence. There's something more happening that I'm missing. It makes the hair on my arms stand on end.

Several times I start a conversation, but it's always stilted and dies off on its own without ever getting going.

We arrive at the City, go straight to the main building, and are ushered in to the Council room, where Visidion and Rosalind are in a deep discussion.

"Welcome," Rosalind says, looking up to greet us as we enter.

Each of us takes a seat around the massive table. Padraig stands beside me, staying close, and takes the seat next to me once I've sat.

Kate lays the stun stick down on the table in front of her with a clatter, and Rosalind's eyes drop to it, then meet each of ours.

Rosalind has a presence to her that commands respect. She's imperious, beautiful sure, but more than that, she's powerful. It's not something I can put into words, but her attitude and her appearance, everything about her screams it.

I try not to draw similarities between her and Annabel but, well I'm not that good.

Visidion is an older Zmaj and reminds me of Gomul a bit.

He sits next to Rosalind with his own quiet control. The aura he gives is every bit the leader as hers is, but he feels quieter.

"The attacks are growing worse," Rosalind says after the greetings are finished. "We know it, now the question before us is what do we do about it?"

"What do we know about them, for sure?" Kate asks.

"They want Tajss," Bashir says.

Helpful Bashir, not vague at all. Everyone glances at him, waiting for him to say more, but when nothing is forthcoming, Rosalind takes the floor back.

"We know they're from off planet," she says, stating the obvious. "They have advanced tech, including weapons. They seem focused on gathering resources, but their attacks have a randomness to them."

"They keep attacking the Tribe," I throw out.

"And the mining settlement," Rosalind enlightens us.

"We've increased patrols," Padraig says. "Drosdan realized they were spying on us and knew when the shield was down. In their last attack the shield was down, their ships were in the air, but they did not bring their guns to bear."

"Then they don't want to risk blowing something up," Visidion says.

"Right," Errol nods. "Our thoughts as well. But what? Do they want the humans?"

"They want secrets," Bashir says. "Tajss hides many things, that is their ultimate goal. They're scavenging what they can, but that is a cover for their true goal."

"What secrets?" Rosalind asks, leaning forward, her hard eyes boring into Bashir. "Their tech is better than ours, what secrets do we harbor that they are after?"

"Ones we haven't yet discovered," Bashir says, shaking his head. "I don't know for sure, I only know that is their goal. That is all which has been revealed to me."

Rosalind purses her lips and leans back. Strangely, I know

that Bashir is right. How or why I don't know, because honestly his words sound like those of a madman. I shouldn't believe him in the slightest, but I do.

"Drosdan had us increase patrols. We're working in pairs, one male, one female," Padraig says.

"You have the women patrolling?" Rosalind asks, her eyes widening.

My skin crawls, and I recoil internally as memories of Annabel leap to the front of my thoughts. I shift in my chair and avoid looking at her. She's not Annabel, and I'm not back where I was. She is her own woman.

No matter how much she's acting like that tyrant.

"Yes," Padraig states matter-of-factly.

"And who thought that was a good idea?" she asks.

"We've been able to manufacture these sticks," Errol says, motioning towards the one lying on the table. "It stuns the Invaders."

"Right," Rosalind says, narrowing her eyes. "A stun stick."

The derision in her voice makes my skin crawl, and I can't bite back the words any longer.

"Would you prefer we remain helpless and at the mercy of everything Tajss throws at us?" I snap.

No one speaks or moves. I don't think anyone dares take a breath. I glare at Rosalind, righteous anger giving me the resolve to meet her steely gaze and not wither.

"Maeve? Right?" she asks.

"Yes," I say, snippily.

She nods, silently assessing me. Her eyes bore into me as if she can weigh my soul with her gaze alone. My resolve wavers under that stare but I fuel it with my low burning rage.

"No," she says, finally. "That is not my concern."

Everyone takes a breath when Rosalind speaks. It's almost one shared gasp of air.

"Then?" I ask, pushing my luck because if nothing else I've gone too far to stop now.

"It is my concern and care that we ensure a future," she says. "Not just our own survival. Visidion and I are in charge of the future of both our races."

"What does that have to do with women joining the Zmaj on patrol?" I ask, confused but not willing to back down.

"Because we have a limited number of females," she says. "Too limited."

Gritting my teeth, I force myself to continue meeting her hard gaze. Inside I want to crawl under a rock and hide, never to emerge. Padraig's hand touches my thigh, and a shiver runs up my spine. He grips my leg, giving me his silent support.

"What exactly does that mean?" I ask, trying to keep the venom from my words that is seething in my thoughts.

The slightest narrowing of her eyes is the only acknowledgment of my vitriol.

"It means what I say," she answers. She blinks then sighs, shaking her head. "I understand how it might seem, but Visidion and I are caring for a longer game than our lifetimes."

Visidion smiles and nods encouragingly. Everyone at the table looks from one to another, and no one here seems to be sure what she's talking about.

She rises from her stool, places her hands on the table and leans towards us.

"Okay?" I phrase my next word carefully.

Inside I'm warring with the chafing nature and reminders of Annabel, but I'm trying to see Rosalind as who she is. A respected leader.

"There has to be a future," she says, motioning around the table with a hand. "A future means there have to be babies. Babies need mothers. Females are the only source of mothers. Currently there are more males on Tajss, Zmaj and Human, than there are females.

Therefore, the females have a higher intrinsic value."

"You can't measure people like that!" I exclaim, rising to my feet.

"I must," she responds, quietly.

"We must," Visidion adds.

"No! That's... wrong! Inhuman, it's reducing a woman down to her womb, and that's not right!"

"No, it's not," Rosalind says. "If that is what we were doing, it would be entirely different than what we are doing. If you think about it, I'm sure you'll understand.

We do not arrange matings or pairings in any manner whatsoever. Nature is allowed to take its course. No one is forcing anything, but there is the inherent need to protect the women."

"Females should be protected," Padraig says.

"I'm not going to be locked up while I wait to be bred!" I yell.

"No one is saying that," Rosalind says evenly.

"You're not? Isn't that the gist of the entire idea?" I can't keep from raising my voice as I look at each of the others at the table.

Kate meets my eyes, but the men don't. The Zmaj obviously agree with Rosalind.

"This is ridiculous," I say. "I can't believe what I'm hearing."

"You're not hearing," Rosalind says. "You're filtering my words through your own, preconceived ideas."

"That's—" I can't form words I'm so angry.

Padraig places a hand on my shoulder, but I shrug it off. He's hurt by the action—I know it because the connection between us throbs with a sudden pain, but I can't spare the attention to it. My anger is jagged in my brain like lightning.

Swallowing, I snap my mouth shut and take my seat.

"If there's nothing else," Rosalind says, waiting to see if anyone else will speak up. "Do we think it's a good idea to put the women at risk like this?"

"We don't have enough men," Errol says flatly. "If we don't, then we won't be able to patrol out as far, safely at least."

Rosalind nods, retaking her seat and looking thoughtful. She and Visidion exchange a long look, and it's obvious that some communication happens between them in that single look.

"Okay," Visidion says. "But please, for all our sakes, be careful."

"We will be," Errol offers.

The rest of the meeting passes, but I barely notice. Seething with anger, I try to look at Rosalind's words through any lens but the one I am. The one that says she's no better than Annabel. That in some twisted, perverse way she's as macho as the Zmaj men. A woman hater.

I only know her by title and rumor from the ship. The Lady General, head of the armed forces. I can't imagine that a woman ascending to such a position on the ship did so easily. The military, even on the ship, was a male-dominated profession, but there were plenty of women in it as well.

Lunch is served while we meet, and while I eat, the food is tasteless. Kate catches my eyes over a forkful and offers a sweet smile. In part, I'm just as angry at her for not standing up with me, but that's not right, and I know it.

At last we escape the meeting room with an agreement to meet later for dinner. We walk out into the evening air. The entire day has gone by, and I couldn't repeat anything that was decided or said after I finally shut up. Padraig takes my hand and I let him, but I'm mad at him too.

I know he has antiquated ideas, all the Zmaj do, well maybe they're not antiquated for them, but they are for humans. Women are not meant, no matter how they try, to be barefoot and pregnant in the kitchen, and there's no way in all that exists I'm going to resign myself to such a fate.

"I'm sorry," Padraig says at last, as we walk along.

"You're sorry?" I ask, looking up.

"Yes," he says, sincerity in his voice.

"For what?" I ask.

He frowns, shakes his head, then stops, turning to face me fully.

"I am sorry I do not understand," he answers honestly. "You are a female, yet you do not want to be honored as such. You deserve to be revered, but you refuse it. I do not understand, but I am trying."

Something in his words breaks through the walls of anger I've erected. I'm left staring at him, speechless. He's never, in all our time together, said anything more raw or more honest.

Smiling, I nod and sigh.

"I know," I say. "I appreciate it, I do, but it's too much. I'm not an object."

"Who would think such?" he asks. "You are you, the most perfect of all the females on the planet. Strong, brave, and with a heart that is full for all around you."

"You're sweet," I say.

"No, it's not sweetness. I say what I see," he replies.

"Okay," I say, feeling awkward.

"What is it that strikes you wrongly?" he asks, taking my hand and we resume walking.

"I don't know."

"Okay," he says, accepting my answer without judgment.

"I'm not a badass, I know it. I don't want to be, but I also don't want to be made less of. My gender shouldn't stop me."

"How would it stop you?" he asks.

"Because of males like you," I say, slapping his arm playfully. "You want to 'put me away' and 'protect' me because I'm a girl."

He laughs and shakes his head. His mirth is contagious and helps to lift my overall bad mood even further.

"Now it is you who does not understand," he says.

"Oh? Then enlighten me, oh male of males, man amongst men," I tease.

"Yes, I will take this task," he says, grinning easily. "I speak from my own viewpoint, one I think most Zmaj share, but it is what I see.

You are a female. We have had no females for... I don't know how long. A very long time, that I do know. We, all of us, had given up. There was no future because we were the last our kind.

When you came, humans I mean, you brought with you hope. Change. A future.

How can we, males that we are, do else but want to protect you? To give you the world? You are everything. With you, there is hope. Without you, we return to staring into the empty abyss that was our future."

"Oh," I say.

His words, though delivered lightly, carry a weight with them. The weight of a future without hope. Knowing you are the last of your kind.

Even after the wreck of the ship, figuring out we were stranded here on this devastated world, none of us faced that. I have no doubt there are lots and lots of humans out there in the universe. Knowing full well we are not the last of our kind and looking at it from that viewpoint gives a weight and a gravitas to it that I've never contemplated before.

"I would never make less of you," he says. "I only want to make more of you. I want you to be my treasure. My heart of hearts. My soul, made whole."

"Oh Padraig," I say, tears falling down my face.

Grabbing his arm, I turn him to face me and rise up onto my toes to kiss him. He returns the kiss fully with barely contained passion made even more evident by his appendage digging into my stomach.

Breaking the kiss, I laugh, letting the last of my indignation go, and wipe away the tears.

"Rverre, no!" a female voice screams.

"Watch, Mommy!" a childish voice answers.

When I look around, I spot a dark-haired lithe woman running down the street towards us.

Her eyes aren't on us, they're fixed in wide-eyed horror at a point over our heads. Following her gaze, I spot what looks like a toddler at least three stories above us, walking along a small ledge on a building.

The building has most of its glass sides missing leaving behind broken shards that reflect the setting suns. The toddler walks along with her arms out to either side, one foot in front of the other, as if she doesn't have a care in the world and there's not a thirty-plus-foot drop to the street below her.

"Mommy, Illadon can't do this," she yells down to her. "See? I'm better. I've got more balance then he—"

A sudden yelp, and she slips.

My heart leaps into my throat, and I can't even cry out as my blood runs cold. I run forward, no idea what I'm going to do, but I have to do something.

The woman running down the street screams, a blood-curdling sound that breaks my heart. The toddler overhead tumbles through the air, and if I didn't know better, because that would be impossible, I'd swear she was giggling.

Padraig runs faster than me with his longer legs, and then he leaps into the air, arms outstretched as he glides towards the tumbling toddler.

Right before he catches her, she spreads her own tiny

wings, and lands lightly in Padraig's arms. The two of them glide to the ground together and now there can be no doubt as to the sound. The toddlers' laughter echoes off the remnants of the buildings around us.

"Again!" she cries out.

"Rverre!" the woman yells, running up breathless.

Rverre wraps her arms around Padraig's neck. He returns the hug, if somewhat awkwardly, but the look on his face I don't miss. After the hug he holds her out to the woman, placing her carefully into her hands.

"Mommy, that was fun!" Rverre giggles.

"No, that was not 'fun'," the woman says. "You could have been hurt, badly!"

"Nuh uh," Rverre pouts, crossing her arms over her chest.

Small nubs of horns stick out of her hair, the light glistens on her scales, and she looks around with great pride.

"Thank you," the woman says, turning her almond eyes to Padraig and me. "I don't know what I would have done if...."

She trails off, not saying the words that would make the worst seem more real.

"It's fine," Padraig answers, tousling the hair of the toddler.

He's so... gentle with her. It's obvious he'd be an amazing father. What am I thinking? Seriously? Me, a mother?

Maybe?

"I'm Jolie, by the way," the woman says, offering her hand to me after transferring Rverre to a hip.

"Maeve," I say, taking her hand.

"I know you, Padraig," Jolie says, smiling. "Thank you again. She's quite the handful."

"I'm special," Rverre pronounces proudly. "Wait till I tell Illadon!"

"How about you don't?" Jolie says, shaking her head. "He gets enough ideas of his own."

"But I'm better," Rverre interjects. "Right, Mommy? Illadon can't go that high. Only me."

"Yes, love," Jolie says. "If you promise to not do it again."

"Why, Mommy?" she asks.

"Because it scares Mommy," Jolie says.

"Oh," Rverre says, looking serious. "Why?"

"Because you could be hurt," Jolie says.

"Your mother is right," Padraig says. "That height, when your wings are not fully formed, it is dangerous."

"It is?" Rverre asks.

"Yes," Padraig says, simply.

"Oh," Rverre says, gazing up at where she was, a calculating look on her face. "Okay."

Jolie sighs heavily, relief flooding her face as understanding dawns on the child.

"Are you coming to the dinner?" Jolie asks, her attention free for us now.

"Yes," Padraig says, cutting off any thoughts I have about it.

Even if I do understand Rosalind's viewpoint, at least in abstract, she still rubs me the wrong way. The entire scene today smacked too much of Annabel and her tyrannical tirades. Sure, I'm probably being petty, but knowing it and changing how I feel about it are two entirely different things.

"Good!" Jolie says with such warmth it cools the fire in my heart. "I'm headed there now if you want to come along."

"Of course," I say, taking Padraig's hand in mine.

We make our way back, and the entire time my thoughts turn over the way Padraig was with Rverre. His massive hands so gentle with her small form. The look on his face, the light in his eyes, the smile in his voice—I can't shake them.

He's so big, massive really, but with her, he was as gentle as an artisan handling the most delicate of glass. There was a softness to him. The more I think about it the more it feels like some internal clock tick and I start to consider, for the first time, a child of my own.

As we sit down to dinner, a communal affair much like we have at the Tribe, I'm at last able to free myself from my fantasies and pay attention to the world around me.

"There are ancient stories of scavengers. Aliens who came to collect relics from Tajss," Visidion is saying from the head of the table. "Old writs and such speak of them. Kalessin spoke of them."

When he speaks, the truth of his words resonates in me, and I know there is something to this. I don't know what, but it's one of those strange moments when I know without knowing how or why.

"Father did?" Padraig asks, disbelief in his voice. "I don't recall him saying anything about them."

Visidion nods.

"Of course, brother," he says.

"What?" I interject, choking on a mouthful of food.

All eyes turn to me as if I'm the only one at the table that had no idea these two were brothers.

"Our Father spoke of them," Visidion offers.

"No, wait," I say, swallowing the food and clearing my throat with a drink. "Brothers?"

Looking between the two of them, my disbelief must be clear on my face.

"Of course," Padraig says, as if this is the most obvious thing ever.

"Yes, Padraig is my brother," Visidion says.

"Then," my mind races with questions and finally settles on one. "Why isn't he in charge of the Tribe?"

"Why would I want to be?" Padraig asks, his voice dropping to an even lower octave, one no voice should be able to hit. It sounds like rocks grinding deep in the earth.

"And that is why," Visidion chuckles.

"Oh," I say, looking at Padraig as if it's the first time I've seen him.

Staring between the two Zmaj, I can see a familial resemblance, and seeing it, I don't know how I missed it. It's like one of those abstract paintings that looks like splatter, but once you see the picture in it, you can't unsee it.

"Visidion and I have discussed the women joining the patrols," Rosalind says, pulling the flow of conversation back to business.

"And?" I ask, arching an eyebrow already bristling at the tone of her words.

"I don't like it," she says simply. "Arming ourselves, that isn't an issue. Sending the women out on patrol creates risks that are unacceptable."

"That doesn't change—" I start, but Rosalind holds up a hand cutting me off.

"No, it doesn't. There are not enough of us. I don't like it, but we have no choice. I have to put my trust in each of you to be smart. Play it safe, and don't engage unless you absolutely must."

Sighing with relief that she's apparently come to her senses at some level, I nod my agreement.

"Good," I say, looking at Kate and smiling.

Kate nods, but doesn't seem enthused by the idea.

"I want as many of these rods made as we can," she says. "Arming ourselves is good. The guns that were salvaged from the ship are mostly depleted with no viable way to recharge them. These are the best advancement we've had in leveling the playing field."

"What about the weapons taken from the Invaders?" Kate asks.

"They're coded somehow," Rosalind grimaces. "They won't fire for us."

"Damn," Kate says, shaking her head.

"How many of these are available?" Rosalind asks, pointing to the stun stick.

"I think there are four right now," Kate answers. "We've got supplies to make a dozen, maybe a few more."

"Right," Rosalind answers, nodding with a thoughtful look on her face. "What do you need to make more?"

"More glass," Errol says. "And metal. As always, there is a shortage of metal."

"The miners," Visidion says. "We'll send messengers to them, see how they're progressing on opening the mines."

"Then that is where we are," Rosalind says with a finality that makes it clear the dinner is over.

There's some small talk, but she and Visidion take their leave in short order. It's not long before Padraig and I are shown to quarters we can use, it being too late to travel back to the Tribe.

It's an actual room, something I haven't slept in since the ship. The bed is still makeshift, a pallet on the floor. Perhaps Zmaj didn't have beds like we did? They're not well-built for them, really, with their wings and tails and such.

"Maeve," Padraig says, his voice soft, touching my shoulders and letting his fingers trail down my arms, eliciting warm chills that race ahead of his touch.

"Yes?" I ask, as he nuzzles my neck.

"You are beautiful," he whispers in my ear, pressing his hardness into my backside.

"You're not so bad yourself," I respond, wiggling against his stiff member.

He hisses, turning it into a growl, as his arms wrap around me and his hands dive in front of me, pressing up against the pounding need between my legs.

I turn my head up to him and our lips meet. We kiss with barely contained passion.

PADRAIG

*P*ounding pulls me from sleep.

"Padraig!" someone yells, and I'm instantly alert, leaping from the tangled covers and leaving Maeve's warmth behind me.

Two steps and I'm at the door, throwing it open. Amara stands there, buxom as always, her hair a tousled mess, face pale. An aura of fear exudes off of her as she pants trying desperately to catch her breath.

"What?" I ask, my scales tingling in anticipation of a fight.

"It's an attack," she says, breathless. "It's massive. They need everyone."

Grabbing my lochaber from where it leans next to the door, I push past her and start for the broken stairway that leads out of the building.

"Keep her safe!" I yell over my shoulder before I step into the dark stairwell.

Leaping down a floor at a time, I reach the bottom fast and emerge into the City street.

Light flashes followed by distant booming sounds, faint

but unmistakable. Overhead there are at least a dozen of the Invader ships firing at the dome over the City.

The dome is holding against their assault without apparent problem but there are a lot of them. How long can it keep up before it fails?

The street around me is empty, so I run towards the City Fountain. Humans emerge from some of the buildings I pass as I run. The males follow in my wake, and some females I don't know come along as well. When I reach the Fountain, Rosalind and Visidion are there already.

"We have a full assault," Rosalind calls out. "They're marching on the airlock. We must keep them from breaking through the dome."

The mass of people around them cries out, not in fear, but in rage. A mix of human and Zmaj voices rising in defiance against those who would invade our home.

"Humans, fall into your teams," Visidion says. "You know who your warleaders are. Follow your Zmaj and listen. Obey their commands and they'll take care of you."

The Zmaj of the City move to stand before the two leaders, Ladon, Astarot, Sverre, and Shidan, moving two arm's lengths apart, and then the humans line up with them.

Some of them have guns, others have makeshift weapons, clubs or long knives. The determination on their faces and in their stance is inspiring. These males are strong, determined, no matter that their bodies are weaker than a Zmaj. They march to face a superior foe without fear.

Admiration grows in my heart for them.

"Padraig!" Maeve's voice cuts over the din of moving people.

My hearts sink, stomach clenches tight, and cold chills race over my scales as I turn. She's running up, Amara at her side.

"No, you must stay behind!" I cry out.

Maeve arches an eyebrow, determination on her face. Amara and she skid to a stop in front of me. Amara has a similar look on her face.

"Oh, you're one of those are you?" Amara asks.

"I'm not hiding out while you go and fight," Maeve says, brandishing one of the stun sticks.

Every fiber of me wants to argue with her. Force her, somehow, to return to safety.

It's wrong. I'm wrong, and I know it.

This is her planet, her home, and she's fully capable of taking care of herself.

The meteorite glass in my chest flashes blue and the glass in her side responds. In an instant I know her thoughts. Feel her determination, her fear, yes, but beyond that fear is her bravery. Her heart and her intention to do whatever she must to save this world. Create a future, with me.

Our eyes lock, boring into each other, and the moment passes. I open my mouth, intending to say something, but there are no words. They've all been said in that instant that we were one. She nods, and I do the same. Turning together we join the forces heading for the edge of the City.

"Well, all righty then," Amara says, joining us.

The edge of the City comes into view and it gives all of us pause. There are hundreds of Invaders closing on the dome. Maybe more. They move across the sand, a beastly blight coming for Draconov.

My dragon roars, the bijass clawing its way forward. The other Zmaj bijass rises as well. I can feel it in the air, echoing around us, laying claim to our thoughts.

No.

I won't give into it. If I'm going to keep Maeve safe, we must work as a team, with all the others. This isn't about simple dominance, this is about survival. Targeting the right enemy and not in a show of brawn.

Rosalind stops at the airlock. She issues orders with sharp commands, her voice carrying easily to all of us. She's smart —her orders are good.

The humans with us mutter. The scent of their fear is heavy on the air. They'll need assurance. A show that we can beat these monsters. That we can win.

An idea forms as the airlock is opened and the units flow out to meet the enemy.

When the door is open the booming sound of the airships assault flows through it and echoes off the buildings. It's deafeningly loud, heightening the sense of fear and concern.

I smile, glance at Maeve, and nod.

"Stay with Amara," I say. "Don't follow me."

"You come back to me," she says, her lips trembling.

"I will," I say. "I promise."

I touch her face and smile as she nods, accepting my words.

As we pass out of the airlock, the warmer air outside brings a sense of life. Roaring, I charge.

Running past the assembling Zmaj and their units. They call to me, but I ignore them. I have to set the tone for them. Show them that these monsters are beatable, vulnerable.

Wings spreading, tail up, spinning my lochaber over my head I race towards the advancing line of enemies.

They fire, and dozens if not more shots slam harmlessly into the sand around me as I dodge from side to side. A couple find their mark, but the distance is enough to lessen the numbing effect.

It doesn't matter, nothing will slow me.

When I'm a dozen yards out I leap, aiming for the biggest one in sight. Lochaber over my head, gripping it with two hands, ready. As I drift down to him, he raises his gun, taking aim. Screaming in defiance, I swing the blade, the full force of my falling form behind it.

The Invader is cloven in two by the force as I land. Blood sprays across me and those closest to him. Time stands still. No one moves or even breathes.

They look at me in horror. Behind their helmets I see their eyes widen in surprise and I can taste their fear.

Roaring, I tear into them. My brethren race to join me, and the battle is joined.

I don't resist my instincts, I embrace them. This is war. They've come to our home, threatened my people, and now they will learn the price.

I'm surrounded by the enemy. They abandon their guns in favor of knives and clubs. They play into my strength.

No matter how good I am, I'm outnumbered. They land their blows even as I drop them. Every time one drops, two more take its place.

Muscles ache, my body slows. The beatings I'm taking are taking a toll. It's hard to breathe. Something swings in from the side, catching a glimpse of it out of the corner or my eye I duck but I'm not fast enough.

The club slams into the side of my head. The world spins. Can't focus my vision. The Invaders around me are a blur.

More blows land. They're piling on top of me, over-whelming, climbing on me like insects on a dung pile.

So much weight, I hold myself upright, unable to swing my arms from the press of their bodies. They climb on top of me, and now someone has an arm around my neck.

My knees quaver, and then I collapse under the weight. My mouth and eyes are full of sand as I'm crushed by the weight of them.

In my head I hear Maeve scream. I can't hear her with my ears, but I know she saw it with absolute certainty.

Maeve.

My female. My promise.

Fighting with all that I have, I get my hands beneath me, feeling sinew tear as I do. Inhaling deeply, I calm the panic and embrace my dragon. Exhaling in a rush I press off the ground.

Muscles tense, pushing, the weight down is more than anything I've ever lifted. Hundreds and hundreds of pounds.

Maeve's face centers my thoughts.

She is in danger.

Roaring, I push harder, and then it breaks. The weight flies off of me, and I explode upright. Free at last.

Invaders land in heaps around me. My lochaber is buried under three of them so I grab a sword from one of the ones scrambling away.

I finish him with a single motion, then set back to my grim work. Cutting through them in a swathe.

A blur of white moves closer, then Rosalind is there beside Visidion. Fighting. The three of us turn our backs to each other, taking on all comers.

Still, they don't stop.

More appear, pouring over the dunes. When I look towards the City, I see Ladon, Astarot, and Sverre are holding the line there. Protecting the women who are fighting as well.

No matter what force they bring to bear, we will not go down. There is no stopping us, because we can't.

We have to win, for our way of life, for our homes, for our families.

The booming sound stops, making the sound of steel on steel louder than any other sound. Up above, the ships are repositioning, apparently giving up on their intent of breaking down the City dome.

"Are they retreating?" Rosalind calls out.

"I don't think so," Visidion responds. "Look!"

The ships, four of them, have moved over the battle. It looks like they intend to bring their bigger guns to bear on us.

"Back into the City!" Rosalind orders.

Those close to the City retreat, but we're too far, and there are too many enemies between us and it.

"Sorry boys," Rosalind says, shaking her head then whirling to block an incoming blade, which she counters with an attack of her own.

Out of the corner of my eye, I watch the retreat while fighting to stay alive here. Maeve passes under the Dome, and a sense of relief passes over me. It's an instant, but all I need. A much needed second wind in the battle. She is safe. No matter what else happens, I have that to cling to.

"Brother!" Visidion yells over the din of clanging steel.

"What?" I ask.

"You remember how angry Mother used to get with us when we were boys? When we came up with that idea to harvest the higher fruit of the baobab tree?"

Busily dodging incoming attacks and sending back out my own I can't give thought to it. It's another memory lost to the fog of the bijass. Something from before, but why is he bringing it up now, of all times?

The whine of the ships is low above us as they move into position. It's obvious that they're no longer interested in fighting us, we're being herded into position.

"Padraig, remember!" Visidion barks.

"You mean—" I duck. "When you'd throw me up?"

"Yes!"

"What of it?" I ask.

"Seems like it might be appropriate," he says. "Right now."

Glancing over my shoulder quickly as understanding dawns on me, I can't stop myself smiling.

"Right, get ready," I answer.

We're going to need some space for this to work so I roar and rush at the line of Invaders swinging their weapons wildly. They scramble backwards, the frontline backing directly into the line behind them, causing confusion.

Stopping my feint, I turn, trusting Visidion to be ready.

He drops to one knee, cupping his hands in front of himself. I run at him. Pushing off the ground, pouring every ounce of strength I have into this desperate motion. If it fails, we're dead. I'll never touch Maeve's sweet face again.

"What—" Rosalind's voice is cut off as my foot lands in Visidion's cupped hands.

He powers himself upright, lifting me with him, and I leap into the air.

My wings catch the hot gusts, so I fly up higher than I ever could on my own, higher than the hovering ship directly over us.

As I crest the front windshield, two unarmored Invaders inside look at me in shock. Leaning into my flight, I reach out and my claws grab the ship.

The slick metal offers no easy purchase. I'm sliding off of it, dropping down as gravity reclaims its ownership.

"NO!" I scream, gripping with all I have.

My nails break, but the steel bends under my fingers, giving me purchase. I'm hanging off the front of the ship by one hand. The nose of it dips down and the engines whine louder trying to compensate for the off-balance weight.

One handhold lets me make another, then I'm lifting myself bodily up the front of the ship. I slam my fist into the protective glass and it bounces off, but I don't give up easily.

Repeatedly I slam into the glass, roaring with rage. Then in a moment of inspiration, I lean closer and belch fire. After the fire spreads across the glass, it spiderwebs when I hit it the next time. On my next hit it shatters, and the pressurized air inside rushes out.

I grab the thing behind the controls, jerk it through the opening, and drop it. It screams, limbs flailing, but I don't have time to enjoy its descent.

The other one is scrambling around, pulling a weapon, which it aims at me. I try reaching for him while climbing through the broken window—I'm trying to get ahold of him before he can fire, but I'm bigger than the opening I bashed in the windshield.

Since I'm stuck partway in, he's able to dance away while I struggle to break the rest of the way in. He fires the gun— this one fires some kind of projectile. It hits my shoulder, ricocheting off my scales and zinging around the tiny cabin.

Blood bursts from his mouth and he drops.

Confused, I force myself the rest of the way in, then move to look at him. There's a hole in his chest and blood pours out of it slowly. He's dead.

Well enough.

Turning my attention to the control panel, I look it over trying to figure out how to fly the thing.

The controls aren't dissimilar to the transport Kate rigged together, which I'm familiar with enough to operate.

This stick must be like the steering wheel. I take the seat, which is uncomfortable, not being designed for a Zmaj, I pull on the stick and the nose of the ship rights itself.

Good.

Pushing it from one side to the other side, the ship responds, and in a few moments I've got a rudimentary grasp of how to maneuver the thing.

Guns. Where are the guns?

The panel in front of me is covered with levers, buttons, switches, and screens. None of them are labeled in any way that makes sense to me.

Fine, if I can't shoot them, I'll show them another way.

As I throw the stick quickly around, the ship spins in

response until I see another of the Invader ships in my sights. Pushing the stick forward makes the whine of the engines increase, and the ship leaps towards it.

Bracing my feet against the floor I keep the stick pushed all the way forward.

A jabbering voice echoes around the cabin, emerging from what must be a speaker.

Ignoring it, I hold my ship steady, ready for the impact that's going to happen. Right before I hit them, I raise the nose just enough to avoid a dead-on hit.

Metal screams as it is forced together, reshaping it as I run over the top of the other ship. I'm thrown forward then back, slamming my head in the process.

Dizzy, thoughts spinning, I work the stick crazily, trying to regain full control of the transport.

The engine sounds off now. Smoke begins filling the cabin, but none of that matters. There are two more ships. I need to take them out before they fire.

The ship jerks then lilts to one side. The speaker resounds with what sounds like screaming. A minor distraction from the work. As it spins around, I spot another one of the ships. Its guns fire. Pulling back, I push the ship to climb. A moment later, the entire thing rocks and shudders around me, taking a direct hit to its under hull.

I push the stick forward and dive towards the ship that fired. They try to move but aren't quick enough. I clip them as I pass, and both our ships are sent spinning.

I'm out of control. The ship is not responding to the stick at all now. There is a webbing material along the ceiling, so I wrap my hands in it, brace my legs to the floor, and prepare myself the best I can for impact.

Sand flies through the broken windshield, and the ship tumbles end over end. I hold myself still for as long as I can, until I lose my grip and I'm thrown around the cabin, slamming into walls, ceiling, then floor in no particular order. Something flies at me and then blackness.

15

MAEVE

"*P*adraig!" I scream.

I don't even recognize my own voice as I struggle to break free of Ladon's grip. Bodily, he hauls me through the airlock. No matter how I fight him, he doesn't let go. He finally sets me free when the airlock has cycled closed behind us.

"They're bringing the ship guns to bear," Ladon says, gripping my shoulders. "We can't be out there."

"Padraig is!"

"I know," he says, staring into my eyes. "I know."

"He's right," Amara says, touching my arm too.

"No!" I cry, tears streaming down my face. "No, I can't... I can't lose him."

"Don't give up on them yet," Ladon says, letting me go and walking away.

Pushing through the milling crowds, I force my way to the dome, where others are watching the fighting. The Invaders surround Padraig, Rosalind, and Visidion. They fight, brilliantly, bravely, but they're outnumbered and alone.

In the sky above, the ships are coming to bear, and it's

clear, even to my untrained eye, that the ground forces are herding the three of them.

There's a soft murmur as more people line up along the wall to watch. The hair on my arms stands on end.

I'm going to witness him die. We've only begun, and now I'm going to lose him.

It can't end like this. I want him. He's mine, we're supposed to be together. Fate, no fate, destiny, whatever, if this is what it all means, then screw all of it!

I can't face this world without him at my side!

Tears fill my eyes, blurring my vision. I wipe them away, trying to bear witness to the horror I know is going to come, but it's futile. Suddenly there's a gasp from the crowd and someone yelps. A cheer erupts.

"What!" I scream.

Why are they cheering? He's dying out there. Alone, without me.

I dry my tears with my shirt the best I can, enough that I can see at least. Visidion and Rosalind face the army alone. Padraig is gone, and my heart breaks. A choked sob slips out as my knees turn to water. Falling against the dome I'm kept up by the weight of the crowd around me.

"Look!" someone screams. "He's on the ship! He's on the ship!"

What?

Someone is pointing up, so I follow the indication, and I see it. Hanging from the front of one of the ships is Padraig. The dome blocks most of the sound, but I see his mouth open and know he's roaring. The sound of it echoes in my head.

He forces his head and arms in and throws an Invader out to tumble to the ground.

The crowd screams with excitement as Padraig forces his way inside the ship. Then he must be in control. It flies around erratically, almost crashes, but then it rights itself. After turning a circle, it races for one of the other ships, ramming it. That ship drops from the sky, but Padraig, through some miracle, continues to fly the damaged machine he's in.

He takes out another of the ships, but this time he doesn't manage to keep his in the air. It tumbles, end over end, until it drops behind one of the dunes. A spray of sand into the air is followed by a pillar of smoke, leaving no doubt that the ship wrecked.

The remaining Invaders turn and retreat as one. The cheering is deafening, hitting a pitch where it becomes a single long blur that leaves my ears ringing.

They're jumping up and down, hugging each other, and everyone is crying. I push through them to reach the airlock. Ladon is punching in the code, and it opens. He looks at me, grimaces, then nods, unwilling to try to forbid me from coming along.

"Come," he orders, taking my hand and dragging me through.

Astarot and Sverre come with us as we emerge out into the open air. The wave of heat makes it even harder to breathe, as if the fear wasn't making it difficult enough.

He has to be okay.

I repeat to myself, over and over, a mantra in my head. He's fine. He's fine.

Racing across the sand, I sink and stumble. Wordlessly Ladon wraps an arm around my chest and helps. Together we move faster, but not fast enough.

His hearts beat in my head but they're erratic, not the steady rhythm I'm used to hearing.

"We have to go faster," I urge. "He's hurt!"

Sverre moves up to my other side, hooks his hand under my arm as Ladon shifts his grip to be the same on my other side. They lift me off the ground and run as only a Zmaj can. The landscape blurs past, Invader bodies lying along our way.

When we crest the dune behind which the ship went down, the smoke plumes into the sky, black and oily. The acrid scent of burning plastic and fuel fills my nostrils.

Fear. Cold hands grip my chest. I'm too scared to cry, to cry out, no sound will emerge from my throat which is clenched closed.

He has to be okay.

The Zmaj carrying me pause for the barest of instances as we come over the top. The ship is a mangled pile of steel twisted into unnatural shapes, resembling nothing of what it did in the air.

Before I can force words, they're moving once more. I'm grateful to them for it, but that's a distant emotion outside the overwhelming worry.

We approach the steel, and they set me back on my own feet. I don't hesitate. Naked flames dance along the metal, burning off whatever fuel the ship ran on.

I know, instinctively, it could blow up. Or there could be an invisible fire, burning so hot my eyes won't see it, but none of that matters.

Padraig is in there, and I have to reach him. His hearts call to me, faint but unmistakable.

When I run to the opposite side, I find a large tear in the hull and climb in. The inside is filled with black, oily smoke that assaults my senses. My body screams for me to run, but I push down those survival instincts.

The heat is incredible. Tajss is hot, always, but this is another level. The metal of the ship being on fire is making this an overheated oven.

Debris lies in jumbled disarray, blocking me from the front cabin. I grab a crate that's half as large as I am, and I strain to lift it. It resists, too heavy for me, but I don't care. I have to get to him.

Ladon climbs in and silently he takes the crate, lifting it with ease and handing it back to Astarot. Together the Zmaj clear a path as I bounce on the balls of my feet, anxiously moving ahead each step as soon as they clear it.

The door to the flight cabin is twisted and bent, hanging on by a hinge. Grabbing it I cry out in pain and surprise. It's super-heated, blistering my hands.

Ladon pushes me to one side, gripping it with both hands. He grunts softly, then jerks and the door breaks free as his muscles bulge then relax.

"Padraig!" I cry out.

A soft groan, then something shifts on the other side of the black emptiness that is all I see beyond the open door. As I start in, a figure emerges.

Padraig grabs onto the doorway, wavers, then pushes himself upright and steps out.

"Get her out," he barks, his eyes widening when he sees me.

Ladon doesn't hesitate, grabbing my waist and jerking me back as he pulls me out of the wreckage.

Outside he doesn't stop. I struggle against his grip futilely until I see Sverre help Padraig out as well. All of us run, putting distance between ourselves and the burning machine.

Only when we're a hundred yards or more away from the wreckage does Ladon stop and set me down. A moment later Padraig, Sverre, and Astarot join us.

"You damn fool!" I yell, stepping up to Padraig's face.

Tears stream down my face, and ,my voice is hoarse from more than the smoke inhalation.

"That was... impressive," Ladon says.

"Impressive?" I scream, turning to face him. "It wasn't

impressive, it was stupid! Foolhardy! He could have been killed!"

"We all would have been killed," Sverre says evenly. "If not for his bravery and fast thinking."

I stop, his words cutting through the raging emotions. He's right, no matter how much I don't want to admit it. Shaking with unvented emotions, tears falling, I sob.

"You could have died," I say, my voice cracking. "I would have been alone."

Padraig wraps his arms around me, protectively embracing me and blocking out the world.

"I promised you," he whispers. "I always keep my word."

"You better," I say, shaking against him.

It's a tender moment but it doesn't last long.

"We should get back," Ladon says, interrupting it.

Padraig squeezes me tight, and then I feel him nod.

When we reenter the City a cheer erupts, and the crowd pushes in towards Padraig, chanting his name. He's a hero, the hero we need, the one we deserve.

He smiles, and shakes hands, and accepts the pats and congratulations with a gracefulness that is surprising. Different from the man I knew such a short time ago. As I watch him closely, I can see that the changes are a definite improvement and reaffirm what I already know.

I love him.

Maybe it's fate. I don't know that I really believe in all that destiny and such, but I do know that humans are survivors. We've survived the crash landing, we've survived Tajss, and for survival to happen there has to be a future worth surviving for. Padraig is that future.

Pride swells my heart watching him receive the adulation and praise he's earned.

That is my man.

At last the crowds disperse as the suns break over the horizon. Exhaustion washes over me like a wave. I'm so tired I can barely keep my eyes open, and as if he knows it, Padraig wraps an arm around me, extricates us from the few remaining people, and takes us back to the room that was assigned to us.

The mat on the floor looks so inviting I want to flop down and pass out, but a deeper, more primal need seeks to be met first.

Grabbing Padraig around the neck, I pull him down into a deep, passion-filled kiss.

"Don't you ever do that to me again," I admonish, leaning back so I can look at him fully.

"Do what?" he asks, a smirk dancing across his face.

"Don't play around—I'm serious," I say.

"I know," he says, lifting me off my feet and pulling me close for another kiss. "I can't promise that though, my love."

"Why not?" I ask, gasping between his passionate kissing.

"Because I will always do whatever I must to keep you safe," he says. "You are my treasure. My everything."

"And you think you're not to me?" I ask, arching an eyebrow.

He smiles, his eyes alight with passion and delight.

"I hope I am," he says. "But if so, you know."

He's right, I hate to admit it, but he is. I would do anything for him. No matter the risk to life or limb.

"Can you promise me one thing then?"

"What, light of my life?"

"Always come home," I say. "Please."

"That I will promise you," he says, suddenly serious.

He sets me down on my feet, looking at me, but his eyes are focused on something distant.

"What is it?" I ask, resting a hand on his chest.

"You," he says, shaking his head and focusing his eyes on me.

"Me?" I ask, confusion in my voice.

"Yes," he says, smiling softly. "When the ship was going down, all I could think of was you. Your face, your touch, the feel of you in my arms. The way you make me feel. Nothing else mattered, in that moment, knowing the trouble I was in, all I could think of was you. Would you be okay? Would I make it back to you?"

"Padraig..." I trail off, unsure what to say.

"You, Maeve, are everything," he says. "My treasure. My claim. All that I want in life."

My cheeks burn as he drops to a knee.

"What are you—"

"Maeve, I want to commit to you, in public. I want you to be mine, forever. Will you commit to me? Forever?"

The world spins away. He's asking me to... marry him? Me? Him?

His eyes bore into me, the smile on his face, the strong lines of his jaw... it all clicks into place, and my heart expands until it feels like my chest will explode.

"Yes!" I cry out, giving voice to the welling storm of emotions. "Yes!"

He explodes to his feet, sweeping me up in the motion, and twirling me around until I'm dizzy. His lips are on mine, across my cheek, kissing down my neck, nuzzling my shoulder.

I drink him in as if he is the sweetest of air. His love washes over me.

The passion turns physical and clothes begin to fly around the room, tossed aside as fast as we can free ourselves of them.

Gently he lays me down on the mat, and then he's kissing across my chest, around the mounds of my breasts and across my stomach.

Welcoming him I open my legs as he lowers himself between them.

When his hot tongue first touches my soft folds I jerk and shudder with delight. Undaunted, he drives forward, working his way into my inner sanctum with a rough, warm, unrelenting tongue.

Diving deep, then dragging up and across my hot pink button that drives me wild with each pass over. He's single-minded in his pursuit of my pleasure, and it builds quickly.

No fold is left unexplored, opened by his hungry tongue, tasted and known fully.

Wrapping my fingers in his hair then sliding to his horns, I grab and pull him in closer. I'm enjoying every instant of his explorations and attention.

I can't help groaning as desire builds higher and the tightness in my core escalates. His tongue drives deep, impossibly so, until I can't take any more, and I fall over the edge into an orgasm that curls my toes and arches my back as I hold him tight against my pussy.

The aftershocks pass with decreasing intensity until I'm left weak and trembling on the mat. He lies down beside me, his fingers softly touching and trailing along my stomach, up to my breasts as he makes soft circles.

His erection rests on my leg, waiting for me to recover, and once I do, I can't wait to be filled by it.

Gripping it softly in one hand, I lean into him for a kiss. Driving my tongue into his mouth, it's my turn to lay claim to him. He groans into the kiss, his need expressing as sound.

Tugging his girth, I break the kiss and make my way down across the hard muscles of his chest. When I reach his cock, I tease the head with my tongue, then run my tongue along the soft underside while playing with his balls.

"Maeve," he moans.

The sound of his voice drives me wilder. I swing a leg

over him, position his cock at my opening, and slide down. His girth expands me.

Throwing my head back, I moan as it slides in deeper until I'm fully seated. Reaching the base, the hard ridge on his pelvis sits perfectly against my clit.

Rotating my hips in a circle makes the pleasure overwhelming. As I build towards another climax, my side warms. I open my eyes and there is a soft, blue glow in the room. When I look down, the meteorite glass on my side is emitting a glow that is echoed by the glass in his chest.

Suddenly everything shifts, and I'm more. More than me, more than us, we're greater than the parts of us, and we're connected, not just to each other, but something bigger.

Much bigger.

Tajss.

We're connected to Tajss itself. The sensation is strange, unusual, but at the same time—right.

An awareness of life across the planet blossoms as we join. Deep secrets call to me, dark points, light points, an awareness of something more.

16

PADRAIG

*T*hrusting into Maeve, giving and receiving pleasure, it grows exponentially.

As I keep looking into her eyes, I can watch the change that comes over her face. She's aware of it as well.

Her warmth grips my member, grasping me firmly, taking and giving to me at the same time.

I hiss with pleasure as the tightness in my core builds, my balls tighten, and at the same time, the connectedness clicks into place, becoming a core part of who and what I am.

Driving in fully, I hold and explode, unable to hold back any longer.

Maeve's fingers clasp around my neck, her back arching up to meet my final thrust as we both cry out our pleasure and climax as one.

After I hold myself up over her, kissing her soft, sweet lips, letting my cock soften inside of her warm walls. Gentle kisses, hot breath—we give to each other silently until at last I'm soft and pull out of her.

She groans as I extract myself and then move to lie next to her. She rolls onto her side, staring, her eyes half-lidded her lips full and pouty. Unable to resist the call of her, I continue kissing her.

"Did you..." she starts, trailing off.

"Yes," I say, knowing exactly what she's thinking.

"So Bashir—"

"Isn't crazy?" I ask, chuckling between kisses.

"Apparently," she says.

"Can I ask you," I start, punctuating each word with another kiss. "I felt something, in you."

She pulls back from my kiss, staring into my eyes, her lips purse and my hearts skip a beat then pound harder waiting for her response.

Can it be?

She bites her lower lips, her eyelids dropping halfway as she looks down and nods.

"Yes," she says, her voice so soft I strain to hear it. Tingles run over my scales. "I think so."

"You're sure?" I ask, breathless.

"No," she says, shaking her head. "Yes. Maybe. I don't know?"

She looks up and meets my eyes. Hers glisten with moisture, and her face is soft, beautiful, perfect in the golden glow of the single candle.

"If not now, then soon?" I ask.

She bites her lip once more, hesitates, then nods.

"I would like nothing more," she says.

I place my hand on her stomach and there's a sudden shock of static electricity. It's followed by an odd warmth and a certainty.

"You are!" I exclaim in a single loud exhale.

She looks down at my hand resting over her womb.

"Yeah," she agrees. "Yeah, I am."

"We're going to be—"

"Parents."

"Yes!" I cry out, leaping to my feet, unable to contain the rush of energy and joy.

She laughs watching me, but my happiness is boundless. I dance around the room excitedly. A child. A future.

I drop to my knees next to her.

"I will protect you, both of you, always," I vow.

"I know," she replies.

"I am yours," I say, leaning in to kiss her.

"And I yours," she responds. "We're yours."

My second cock rises so fast and hard it's painful. She doesn't miss the reaction. Her hand is on it in an instant and she strokes it softly.

"Always," she says.

A groan is all the response I can give as she tightens her grip and goes to work on my member. Spinning her legs around and placing them on either side of me she leans back on her arms, inviting me home.

I don't hesitate to lay my claim.

MAEVE

"*U*nfortunately, the Invader ships that were downed during the conflict were destroyed," Rosalind says.

"It'd be great to have one of them to study," Addison says. "Who knows what we could salvage from it."

There is a round of agreement around the table, but the situation is what it is.

"There seems to be no doubt now that the Invaders are scavenging with a particular interest in the meteorite glass," Visidion says.

"Right," Ladon says. "Though they do not seem averse to collecting anything that gets in their way. They're still not using deadly force. Clearly they want captives."

Silence falls over the council room when he says this. My heart pounds just thinking about it. Instinctively, my arms cross my belly protectively.

"There is little we can do about that," Sverre says. "What we can do is prepare ourselves for more attacks. We need to coordinate better than we have."

"Agreed," Rosalind says. "We don't have enough manpower."

"Yes, we're spread thin, but what would you propose?" Padraig asks.

"Our options are limited," Visidion responds. "If these attacks continue at this rate, we might consider consolidating our resources."

"Consolidating?" Padraig asks.

He's bristling inside, and barely contained anger races through my body too, making the hair on my arms stand up.

"Yes," Visidion nods.

"You mean, move the Tribe?" Padraig asks.

"It is a sensible solution," Sverre inserts.

"No, it's not," Padraig answers through gritted teeth. "How, in all your wisdom, do you propose to feed everyone?"

"We have made progress on growing food here in the City," Rosalind says.

"Progress? Has this been the goal the entire time?" Padraig asks, his eyes locked to Visidion.

"No," Visidion answers, meeting Padraig's glare without flinching. "It is a topic of discussion, that is all."

"Then it's a stupid idea," Padraig says. "The Tribe is not going to agree to move into the City."

Visidion nods as Rosalind sighs. He places his hand over hers where it rests on the table.

"It would be a temporary measure," Rosalind says.

"I'm sure it would," Padraig says, dismissive.

"Padraig," Sverre says. "Do not let prejudice cloud your judgment. It is only up for discussion for the good of all of us."

"And I said no," he says, shifting his glare to Sverre.

Ladon crosses his arms over his chest and harrumphs.

"I said he would be this way," Ladon says.

Out of nowhere, I'm so angry I can barely contain it. Red

rage fills me, and I rise to my feet at the same time that Padraig does. As one we place our fists on the table leaning towards Ladon.

"Say it again," Padraig hisses.

It's not my anger, it's his. This is what he and the rest of the Zmaj must deal with, the bijass they barely speak of. It's horrifying how fast it hit him, and through him, me.

Taking control of myself, easy enough because it's not really my rage, I place a hand on his shoulder. His head jerks towards me, rage burning in his eyes.

"Padraig," I say, keeping my voice soothing.

He glares at me, for a long enough moment that I wonder if I'm getting through to him, then he nods and resumes his seat.

"Fine, discuss," he says, hitting the table with fist. "The answer is no, but feel free to talk until you're blue."

The other Zmaj at the table look to Rosalind and Visidion.

"Well, that's good enough for that," Calista says, smiling. "Let's table that for a last resort, huh?"

"Agreed," Rosalind responds.

Discussion roams around with other strategies being discussed on how to best protect ourselves from the Invaders. It's long and boring. I'm having a hard time focusing my attention on it, as it seems we're arguing in circles, getting nowhere fast.

There's a sound outside the door, and then it opens. A haggard-looking man stumbles in with a woman at his side.

"Jackson? Tessa?" Rosalind asks, rising to her feet.

The man holds up a hand, gasping. The girl with him is doing the same.

"One... minute," he says, hands on knees as he struggles to catch his breath. "Ran up, all the stairs, and here..."

Silence so deep I could hear a pin drop covers the

room as we wait, the only sound the two people gasping air. Jolie gets water for the two which they take gratefully.

"Okay," Jackson says at last, straightening. "Yeah. There was another attack on the settlement."

"Was anyone hurt?" Rosalind asks, her first question.

I look over at her with a changing of my estimation of her. Her first concern was for the people, not the settlement. There's an aspect to her voice that was more... human than I'd expect.

"No," he says.

"Not badly," Tessa adds. "Some damage, nothing too serious."

"Good," Rosalind responds, relief in her voice.

"We got one," Jackson grins, looking at Rosalind.

"One?" she asks the question we all have.

"Yes!" Tessa exclaims. "We downed a ship."

"And it's not destroyed?" Ladon asks.

"No, it's banged-up, but we got it!"

Conversation erupts as everyone begins talking at once. It grows to a crescendo when Rosalind calls us to order.

"Enough!" she barks. "Jackson, well done. Thank you for bringing this to our attention."

Jackson nods, accepting the gratitude and the pats on the back from those in the room.

"I need to transport it here," Addison says. "It will be easier to investigate here with my lab close to hand."

"Okay," Rosalind nods, looking at Padraig and me. "Can you two lead a team to bring the downed ship back here?"

"Yes," Padraig says without hesitation.

"Good," Rosalind says. "Everyone give whatever help is necessary."

The meeting continues for a while longer, but the mood has been elevated by the good news brought by the miners.

After it finally disperses, Padraig and I have our first chance to talk since the previous night.

"Are you okay?" I ask, thinking back to his instant rage.

"Of course," he says.

"You can't lie to me, you know?" I smile at him. "Not even a little bit."

He looks down into my eyes, hesitates, then nods.

"It's something I've been concerned about since Visidion and Rosalind became mates," he answers me honestly.

"What about it?" I ask.

"He's my brother. I am happy for him to have found his mate. I am more than happy that you humans came to our planet. None of that mitigates the fact, I don't want the Tribe to lose its identity. I do not want us to be absorbed into an amalgamation of the City."

I nod, thoughtfully.

"The customs here are different," I observe.

"Yes," he agrees. "The human culture rules here. The Zmaj here have accepted this. That is fine, for them. It is not what I want for our future."

"I see," I say, feeling lost.

He senses it and stops walking, taking my hands in his.

"Maeve," he says. "Please understand. A new future, a blend of our cultures, this I can support. What we have at our caves, with the Tribe, it is precious to me. As it is.

Do you not see how different it is here? Nothing here is like it is at our home."

Pursing my lips I think it over. In a way I see his point. The City is different. It's familiar to me mostly because it is very similar to how life on the ship was. There's community, yes, but it's a more distant sense of community.

The Tribe has more a familial sense to it. There is an easy camaraderie that the City lacks. It's more like a family is the best I can put it into words. The City is more like, close neighbors. All friendly, all working together, but not above personal concerns as much.

"Yeah, I get it," I say. "But... the Tribe has a distinctive human influence. Are you sure you're okay with that?"

"Of course I am," he says, lifting my hands to his lips and kissing each of them in turn.

"Good," I grin. "You're stuck with me, you know."

"I would not have it any other way," he says.

The meteorite glass in my side pulses softly and I know he's being honest with me. The connection we share seems to be growing stronger somehow. It's almost telepathic but not quite. Yet. Will it get there? I don't know but if it does, I don't think I'll mind.

"Let's get to work," I say. "Apparently we have to figure out how to transport a ship back here."

"Of course, my love. With you, all things are possible."

MAEVE

"*I* think it's perfect," I say to Penelope.

The makeshift Christmas tree she's made is unique, different, and very abstract but beautiful. It does convey the idea considering it's constructed of scrap metal, bits of plants, and some twigs decorated with meteorite glass. The glass sparkles, reflecting the candle light. An entire wall of the main cavern has been dedicated to the celebration.

"Thank you!" she responds.

"So, when is everyone supposed to get here?" Delilah asks.

"Soon," Penelope smiles.

"Zoe, you have to wait my love," Olivia says, grabbing the toddler and pulling her away from the plainly wrapped gifts lying under the tree.

We don't have colored paper or the resources to make it, so the gifts have been wrapped with pieces of leather or scraps of cloth.

It doesn't matter one bit. In fact, it's better this way. Every piece under that tree is exactly what it should be. Each person, I know, has put a lot of thought and consideration on top of their own effort to create what they are presenting.

Cupping the tiny swell of my belly I hum softly. The meteorite glass embedded in me thrums in time with the tune. Addison doesn't think there will be any complications from the glass, though she wants to monitor the pregnancy closely. I want her to, nothing can go wrong, but the idea that it will is distant. Barely worth considering. I know, with that strange certainty I'm learning to accept, that it will all be fine. The planet wants this baby, almost as much as Padraig and I do.

Bashir stops as he walks by, his eyes locking with mine as if he knows my exact thought at that moment. He smiles, nods, then resumes his trek, carrying a large load of cooked meats to the serving table.

The scent of the roasted meat makes my mouth water, reminding me how hungry I am. I've never been sure about the whole 'eating for two' thing among pregnant women, but now I do know, and I swear I could eat an entire guster by myself.

"They're here!" Olivia calls from the cave entrance.

Excitement runs through the air, electric, as we rush out to welcome our guests.

Almost all of the City and several people from the Mining Settlement trek through the gates and into the open area enclosed by the wall. Rosalind and Visidion are in the lead but with them are all the parents from the City.

Ladon and Calista with Illadon, Jolie and Sverre with Rverre, Shidan and Amara with Malcolm who is desperately trying to keep up with Illadon and Rverre. The older two children mostly ignore the younger, playing some game of their own.

Ryuth steps out of the transport and reaches in to help Mei out. Each of them carry a tiny bundle crooked in one arm. My heart flutters seeing them both. It's the first time they've come back to the Tribe since the birth of the twins.

Drosdan races past the new arrivals to the transport, ignoring all of them. Leaning his head disappears into the dark portal of the open door.

"What is he doing?" I ask aloud.

"You didn't hear?" Delilah asks.

"Hear what?" I ask.

"Sarah's coming too," she smile.

"Isn't she due like, any day now?"

"Yup," Delilah snorts. "He's not happy she left the City but apparently she insisted."

Astarot assists Drosdan and together they lift a chair out of the transport. Sarah sits on it, for all the world a Queen on her throne. She smiles, squinting at the bright light of the world. She glows with life and excitement.

Rosalind steps over to speak with her as well as Calista and Jolie, all making sure she's okay, it would seem. She shoos them away, rising to her feet once the chair is on solid ground and embracing Drosdan.

Strangely enough, I feel the connection between the two of them, not as strongly as I do the one between Padraig and me, but I'm definitely aware of it.

Sarah resumes her seat, and the two Zmaj carry her into the main cave past Delilah and me.

Dinner is ready to serve, so everyone makes their way into the cave, finding spots at the long communal tables. We've moved the tables to form a U shape. Rosalind and Visidion sit at the head table along with Ladon, Calista, Drosdan, and Sarah. Two humans join the table at Rosalind's insistence. It takes me a moment to recall their names but when I do it makes sense.

Jackson and Tessa are the leaders of the Mining Settlement, more or less, as much as they have a leader.

We've all heard the stories of Gershom and his... what? His idiocy? Craziness?

Ah well, what can we say, my group has Annabel, they have Gershom. Apparently one out of every ten or so humans is a wannabe tyrant, given half a chance.

Chuckling, I mention that to Delilah who gets a kick out of it. Food and drink flows freely, including the fermented britang, which keeps the mood even lighter. I pass on that, of course. No matter how certain I am that my baby will be fine, no point in being stupid about it.

As the meal comes to a close, Rosalind and Visidion rise. She taps the table lightly, calling everyone's attention. It takes a few moments before the buzz of conversation ends, and everyone is looking to her.

She smiles, and for the first time I see a beauty in her austere looks. She's a hard woman. I guess you would be if you'd lived her life, but there is a genuine warmth to her. The sharp lines of her jaw and facial structure light up as she looks around the room, holding a cup in one hand.

"Everyone," she says, her voice carrying easily to all of us. "Thank you for being here."

An echoing response comes to her statement, and she waits for it to pass.

"It has not been easy," she continues. "Our road has not been what any of us expected. It is a testament to our spirit, Human and Zmaj, that we have not only survived, but that despite it all, we've flourished.

"So today, I welcome you to our first celebration. A planet holiday, a tradition melding ones from our past with ones of our native protectors.

"Let it be celebrated from now until the end of time. This is a time of giving. Giving of gifts, yes, but more than that. This is a time of giving thanks. In our exchange, to begin soon, let us give our gratitude. One to another, sharing the work of our hands and let us never forget that together we are stronger."

The applause and cheers are deafening, echoing off the stone walls in response to her words.

I wipe away tears from my eyes, my emotions getting the better of me.

"Are you okay?" Padraig whispers in my ear, though his whispering is still loud enough everyone close to us hears his rumbling voice.

"Yes," I sniff, trying to stem the rising tide of emotions.

"Are you sure?" he asks, concern in his voice.

Looking up and meeting his eyes, I can't answer with words because my throat closes tight. Smiling, I kiss him instead, showing him rather than saying that I am fine.

"Presents now, mommy?" Illadon's soft voice carries loudly having spoken in a moment of overall silence.

Laughter erupts as everyone looks at the young boy.

Everything is perfect. More than perfect. It's exactly what it should be. All of us coming together. Humans, Zmaj, the children, coming together and sharing as a community.

We go over to the makeshift tree, decorated with shiny bits of glass that couldn't be better. There's so much love put into the creation of that tree it feels like it flows out to all of us as we move seats to sit in a semicircle around it.

The children are restless, looking at the packages, Illadon and Rverre dance from foot to foot watching each other and their mothers, waiting, if not patiently, for permission.

"Okay," Calista says.

Jolie smiles broadly. "Go!"

That might as well have been a starters' gun. The two race towards the presents followed closely by Malcolm who struggles to keep up with them. Zoe tumbles as she races behind him, but she rolls, coming to her feet and toddling on forward.

Each of them grab a present, lifting it up and looking at it closely. Illadon looks at the other children, his tiny face imperious.

"Okay," he says, his voice serious. "Each of you take one gift to one person."

He gives orders easily and surprisingly, though perhaps it shouldn't be, the other children listen. As one they nod their understanding and walk with their chosen package to one of the adults sitting in a circle. In quick order, under Illadon's exacting direction, the presents are distributed.

His leadership is clear. Even Rverre listens to him, and I've seen how the two of them challenge each other in their normal course of play.

Once all the presents are distributed evenly, Illadon's face breaks into a big smile. He looks quickly at his parents, who nod, and he laughs.

"Now!" he yells, dropping to a sitting position and ripping the package in his hands open.

Everyone opens their gifts, and I follow suit. Inside my package is a decorative mobile made with bits of meteorite glass and colored rocks. When I hold it up, I see the dangling parts hang from cured sinew. It catches the light and sparkles beautifully. It will be perfect over a crib.

I look at Padraig and hold it up, smiling broadly. He tilts his head to one side, staring at it, then he smiles too.

"Oh," he says. "It's decor!"

"Yes, silly," I say. "What did you think it was?"

He looks sheepish and shrugs. "I did not know."

"It's okay, I still love you," I say, kissing him to make sure he knows I'm teasing.

The buzz of conversation rises, and everyone is happy with their various gifts. The children set about playing with the things they've gained, and some folks trade their gifts for things more to their interest.

After a while musical instruments are brought out, and

songs begin along with dancing. We drink, we eat, and we make merry.

It's a successful Christmas. No one brings up the Invaders, not even once. They're a problem for tomorrow. Today is about us. At long last we're doing more than surviving. We're living.

The party goes late into the night until we find berthing for all of our guests and at last, exhausted, Padraig and I are alone in his room.

"Are you happy?" he asks, hands on my waist, his face close to mine.

"Yes," I say. "More than I ever thought I could be."

"Good," he murmurs, kissing my neck.

"Are you?" I ask.

"What more could I ask for?" he says, his words each accented by a kiss.

"I don't know," I muse. "You're a very lucky dragon. I'm quite the catch."

He snorts then raises his head to meet my eyes.

"You are," he says, seriously. "You are everything."

"I love you," I say, and my heart expands so much I'm sure my chest is going to explode, unable to contain the depth of my emotion for him.

"I love you," he says.

He steps away and turns his back. He lowers himself to his knees and reaches under the bed. When he turns back around, he has a package in his hands. He holds it between us, shifting around and barely meeting my eyes.

"I did not," he begins and stops. "No, I do not understand your tradition."

"It's okay, we're making a new one," I answer him.

He meets my eyes and smile.

"Yes," he agrees. "Yes. I didn't understand it, but I do like the idea. Giving a gift is a unique way to show what you feel."

He holds the package out and I take it from him. He's nervous. It's not something I can see as much as I feel it.

"Thank you," I say.

He stares at the package in my hands waiting with silent anticipation.

"I hope you like it," he says, his deep bass voice softly caressing my skin with the lightest of touches.

Slowly I open it, taking great care because my heart is pounding so hard my hands are trembling. As the leather wrapping falls away I'm left holding the most beautiful thing I've ever seen.

Looking from it to Padraig, tears fill my eyes. My throat clenches shut, unable to give voice to the overwhelming love that fills me.

In my hands is a heart. It's made of metal beaten out so thin and delicately that it feels like the finest of glass. Decorating it are tiny pieces of meteorite glass. It's slightly smaller than the palm of my hand and mounted with a leather cord so I can wear it around my neck.

"I wanted you to give you a representation of what you have," he says.

"Your heart," I answer, my voice squeaking as I force words past the blockage.

He nods, pursing his lips, waiting.

Trembling, I meet his eyes, and can't hold back the tears. So much love explodes out of me I'm crying, laughing, and sobbing all at the same time. Gripping it tightly in my hand, I throw my arms around his neck and kiss him.

He lifts me off my feet, holding me tight, our lips locking together until I stop trembling and the tears slow at last.

"It's perfect," I say, as he sits me back on my feet.

I slip it over my head and the heart hangs perfectly between my breasts, his heart covering mine.

His smile is radiant, lighting up the room in the same way it lights up my heart.

"I love you, always, forever," he says. "My heart is yours; I am yours."

"I'm yours," I respond.

We embrace, kissing with barely contained passion. As we snuggle into bed, the exhaustion of a long day on us, his body encompasses me. Holding me tight and protective.

Trillions of miles, random chance encounter with space pirates, a shipwreck that never was supposed to happen. Surviving that, monster attacks, Invaders, and everything that stood against us ever finding each other, none of it matters.

Love finds a way.

THE END

ABOUT THE AUTHOR

USA Today Bestselling Author of fantasy and scifi romance, Miranda Martin's books feature larger than life heroes with out-of-this-world anatomy and smart heroines destined to save the world. As a little girl she would sneak off with her nose in a book, dreaming of magical realms. Today she brings those fantasies to life and adores every fan who chooses to live in them for a while.

She was born and raised in southern Virginia, but as a veteran she's traveled to places like Korea, Hawaii and good 'ole Texas. Now she's settled in Kansas, the heart of America, with her husband and daughters. Her favorite animals are dragons, unicorns and cats. If she's not writing, you can still find her tucked away somewhere with a warm blanket and her nose in a book.

Get in touch!
mirandamartinromance.com
miranda@mirandamartinromance.com

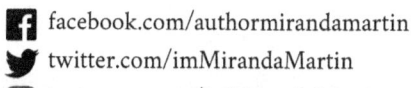

facebook.com/authormirandamartin
twitter.com/imMirandaMartin
instagram.com/imMirandaMartin